Squeeze

Dragon Point

Eve Langlais

New York Times Bestseller

Copyright

Prologue

Somewhere in a little town that used to be sleepy…

I think the Lytropia Institute is doing bad things. Very bad and illegal things. Not unusual in the cutthroat field of medicine. Everyone wanted to get ahead, to be the one to discover the next billion-dollar idea.

In that respect, Lytropia wasn't any different. The medical building had secrets. Lots and lots of secrets. Some of them broke laws—and crossed ethical boundaries.

What to do?

The video footage someone had sent by email proved they were engaged in less than savory practices, and there was no disguising the fact that, in the video, the owner of the institute appeared quite clearly. Even clearer was the fact that someone—or something—was being held prisoner. Not anywhere public, though.

A search of the simple, three-story lab and office building didn't reveal any hidden rooms or off-limits sections. That were above ground, anyway. But rumors, more like whispers really, claimed that the institute didn't stop at the first floor, but rather stretched below the surface.

Underfoot, where no one could see.

More gossip hinted at level after level of hidden labs and cages. Cages with things inside, not quite human things. By nature or design?

Did someone play God with lives?

It seemed so, and yet, the outside world didn't know that. Didn't even suspect. They thought the institute, once a place for mental patients and left derelict for decades, was a place of higher understanding. Owned and operated by the emerging shapeshifters of the world, it was involved in the study of the Lycanthrope genome, trying to discover what made a werewolf a were. How could their body reshape as it did, heal so much quicker…? If they could figure it out, then the application of that knowledge to certain physical ailments would be mind-blowing.

Healing wasn't the only thing the institute was researching. The Lycan people had amazing hair, and they could almost literally grow it overnight if they chose. There was incredible interest from the follicular industry as to possible uses for curing baldness.

The Lytropia Institute and its testing of shapeshifters should not be mistaken or compared to the now defunct Bittech Facility. That corporation had dissolved within the last few months. The three labs it had operated were shut down and cleaned out when Parker—a real slimy piece of work—disappeared suddenly after his niece's birthday.

To those who'd somehow managed to ignore the news and crazy revelations of the past nine months, Parker was the werewolf who'd outed shapeshifters and all manner of other non-human beings to the world.

Not everyone took it well. Especially those suddenly thrust into the limelight. Apparently, the shapeshifter community—or was that packs?—were quite happy hiding in the shadows. Pretending they lived a perfect Cleaver life with a white picket fence. Just ignore the fact that they didn't own a dog and yet erected a doghouse out back with heating and cooling and all kinds of fancy amenities.

Shapeshifters had gotten shoved out of the closet, and not all humans had reacted well to the news, which, in turn, meant many people were mad at Parker. Even more people were scared of him. What would he tell the world next? What devious things did he plot?

Parker and Bittech appeared gone, but did that mean the experiments they'd conducted ceased, too?

No one knew for sure. Bittech didn't leave behind any clues. But wow was its shutdown worthy of a convincing conspiracy theory.

The whispers said cover-up. The dark armored vehicles with no plates, no identifying marks at all, arrived under cover of darkness. The day after Parker vanished, someone swooped in to the Bittech facilities when most people slept—a huge convoy seen by only a few. The videos uploaded showed a stream of tail and headlights snaking to the institute's remote locations outside three towns.

Most people went back to bed rather than investigate. They missed all the action. In the morning, the trucks were gone, as was everything inside Bittech. Nothing got left behind. Or so the media reports claimed as the reporters and their cameramen wandered the buildings, the office, and the lab spaces barren of anything, especially clues.

Lytropia Institute—often shortened to LI— was not Bittech. The shifters who owned the building and created the facility never hid their purpose. They'd explained from the beginning, "We are dedicated to discovering the secret to being a werewolf." They were very candid because they'd seen the backlash caused by Parker and the experiments he'd condoned—genetic experiments on unwilling hosts.

LI didn't experiment, though. Not on humans or other shifters, at least. They studied things like tissue and fluids, putting them under microscopes, injecting them with various elements to trigger reactions.

Perfectly harmless stuff.

If LI is so aboveboard, then what are they hiding so far below ground?

Did they play with things best left alone? Who to tell? And what to tell? An accusation required accurate information because what if there was a logical explanation? Perhaps the company had the proper permission from the government to play with the lives of others.

I need the truth. Infiltration was required, but that required skills to get past the barriers in the way. Someone tech savvy, who could penetrate firewalls and sift through files undetected. If someone could thrust right into the heart of the enemy, perhaps they would emerge with the secrets needed to answer the eternal question: *Is Lytropia doing good or evil?*

And what could be done about it?

Chapter One

"This is the place. I can feel it in my gut."

"You felt that in the last place we raided, too," her cousin remarked. "Turns out it was all that hot sauce you put on your tacos."

Fire in the hole. And then back out. The warning on the label obviously didn't exaggerate about the burn. "Eating is like working out. Sometimes, it hurts. But it was so worth it." The heat in her mouth, the salty tang of the cheese, the rich sweetness of the salsa, the seasoned meat complemented by the guacamole. Pure heaven. She'd have added the whole operation to her hoard if she could. But, apparently, kidnapping food truck owners to cook for her at any time of the day was considered confinement. Humans and their laws—such spoilsports.

"I can't believe they shut Pedro down." Deka shook her head. "He made the best chalupas."

"He did." Such a shame he had to close, not for health violations but illegal importing. Who knew there was a market for smuggling banned hot sauce into the country?

Good thing Adi had snared a few cases before the FDA confiscated and destroyed the recovered stash.

"Wish I had one of his chicken tacos and a half-dozen chalupas right now." Deka rubbed her tummy and jutted her lower lip in a formidable pout. "We shouldn't have skipped dinner."

"We'll grab a snack after we're done." And by snack, Adi meant hitting the nearest diner and ordering everything on the menu, except for the salads. All that green and healthy stuff just got in the way.

"I say we're already done. There's nothing to see." Deka pointed from her spot, a good vantage only a few dozen yards outside the walled compound, with a perfect line of sight to the now derelict building. Her spot was also up a tree. But given the fall weather, most of the branches were bare. Perfect for perching.

Adi poked at her cousin. "You want to leave before checking it out? Are you kidding me? Look at it. It's perfect." She pointed to the building, its windows dark, the grounds appearing lifeless.

"If by 'perfect' you mean abandoned…"

"What better cover if you were experimenting illegally?"

"*If* being the key word. Maybe there was some hinky stuff going on, but according to our dossier on this Bittech place, the government cleared the building out last week. There's nothing left."

"Or so they want you to think. I call bullshit." Adi flung the curse with gusto, not afraid at all—because Aunt Yolanda wasn't around with her bottle of castor oil. She didn't recommend gargling it, and if you swallowed, expect the fishy burp twenty minutes later. "You and I both know how easy it is to cover things up."

Deka groaned. "Not with the conspiracy thing again. Weren't you paying attention in our theology class? If it quacks like a duck, then chances are, it is a duck, and we should bring it back to Cook so he can glaze it."

"Deep fry."

"Whatever. The point is, this is just an abandoned building. Nothing more."

"If it's so abandoned, then why is there such a loss of electricity in this area? Did you know the average neighborhood only has a loss of four to six percent energy during distribution? But here, it's almost four times that. Almost as if something massive is siphoning from the grid."

"When Aunt Waida's nephew on her husband's side was growing those pot plants and borrowing electricity from the neighborhood, they noticed right away because everyone's bill suddenly went up. So don't you think they would have investigated something happening here and shut it down?" Deka queried.

"That's what usually happens, but in this case, no one noticed because those living in the area aren't being billed for it." But the raw meter readings she'd gotten her digital fingers on didn't lie. "Whatever is sucking up the juice was still at it as of two days ago." Adi couldn't help a satisfied smile at her awesome sleuthing skills.

Deka shook her head instead of being impressed. "How do you know these things?"

Because Adi knew where to poke her nose. "You may bow before my greatness."

"You wish. So let's say I believe you, and there is something sucking the power…" Deka made obscene slurping noises because she lacked technique. "Then where is it? This place doesn't have any other buildings large enough to house another lab. Not a secret one at any rate."

"It's here." Adi pointed. "I'll bet you a case of Twinkies"—from her precious hoard—"that this place has an underground lab just like that Bittech place did in Florida."

"And how do you plan to get into it? The military sealed off the building."

"Watch and learn, dear cousin." With a move a gymnast would applaud, Adi did a loop on her branch and dropped out of the tree, landing with her knees slightly bent and her arms outflung in a flourish. Style couldn't be ignored.

With a tilt of her head, Adi addressed her cousin still perched above. "Are you coming, or will any treasures I find belong to me alone?"

"Heifer. You'd better share. I gave up a season premiere with that hunky demon fellow to follow your ass."

Adi blew a spraying wet raspberry. "Oh, please. You never watch live television anymore. And besides, even you have to admit this is much more exciting. We aren't getting any younger." Tick, tock. Soon, she'd find herself grounded and bored.

Throwing herself backwards off the branch, Deka flipped in the air and landed on her feet. "And the crowd goes fucking wild!" she crowed, holding her hands in the air and cheering.

It would be more impressive if it was a rare gift; however, all the dragonesses in the Silvergrace family possessed agility and grace. In order to keep themselves in shape, they had a ballroom at home with swings at impossible heights that they practiced leaping from—and no nets to catch them.

Aunt Yolanda always had splints on hand for the few times they'd failed as youngsters. Even the most painful break didn't frighten them off. They got right back up there, swinging and leaping. Even in a cast, the girls would practice because, as her mother said when Adi's sister Aimi dared to complain, "Think of the cast as the weight of your enemy clinging to you. He will try to bring you down. You must adjust for this. And then crush him." *Crack.* She could still hear the smack of her mother's fist against her palm.

Welcome to Adi's world. Her mother didn't bake cookies, drive them to soccer practice, or belong to the PTA. Her mother was cutthroat in real life and in business. Not that anyone ever found the bodies. What bodies? Investigations never turned up anything, and so what if the convenient disappearances meant that their empire grew? Mommy dearest protected the family—it was the most treasured thing in her hoard. #dontfuckwithfamily.

Adi bent over and grabbed the bag she'd stashed at the foot of the tree. "I brought a few tools to give us a hand getting inside."

"I don't suppose you've got a ladder in your bag of tricks?"

"No, but I do have rope." She patted the heavy canvas sack and grinned. "I've also got handcuffs, in case we get lucky."

"Throw in some lube, and it's a party," Deka

muttered.

"Speaking of, let's get this party started." Restraining an urge to whistle, Adi headed toward their target.

The first layer of protection was a ten-foot stone wall. Deka knelt and offered a hand to spring Adi. She stepped lightly into her cousin's laced fingers, and as she was propelled upward, she grabbed the rough lip of the barricade and hoisted herself onto it. As she sat up, the bag swished past her face, narrowly missing her. It hit with a thump on the other side.

She made a noise. "You missed."

"Pity," Deka muttered. "Give me a hand because I am not ruining my manicure on this wall."

Adi maneuvered herself onto her belly and dangled down, her hand outstretched. Deka jumped, and their fingers linked, the jolt making Adi grumble. "I'm going to have a stone-speckled belly." Really not a sexy look. Right up there with plastic waffle lounge chair butt.

"Stop complaining and pull."

"Have you been hitting that donut place for breakfast again?" Adi huffed.

"Yes."

"And you didn't bring me any? You are so demoted from favorite cousin spot."

"Cough up some dough to buy some, and maybe I'll bring you some back. Or, even better, trade you for some of your cakes."

"Never." Adi didn't believe in sharing. *It's my hoard.*

Sitting on the wall, they took a moment to

survey the inner yard. The very quiet and dark yard.

There was something kind of disappointing about scaling a wall and dropping down to the other side without getting attacked by dogs or caught by guards with bright flashlights. It made a mockery of her effort to look hot as part of her plan to distract while she kicked ass.

The second gate, about ten feet from the first, was comprised of chain link and barbed wire at the top. A sign cautioned them about the electrical voltage.

Adi reached out and touched the cold metal. Nothing jolted. "The power's off on the fence."

"Good thing, or you'd have hair like Babette did when she tangled with that electrical eel off the barrier reef."

Such an awesome family vacation. Sun, sand, and every night for dinner, sushi. The poor villa chef had quit cooking because they kept refusing to eat the lavish suppers he prepared them. Not their fault they ate al fresco in the ocean.

Deka poked her fingers through the mesh and began to climb. "I hate barbed wire. It's hell on my leggings."

"Then good thing I brought some tools."

Adi patted her leather jacket—genuine, she might add, because the artificial kind offended the predator in her. The interior pocket held wire cutters and a whistle—in case she got bored waiting for some action to find them.

Click. Click. She created an opening while Deka kept watch—of her phone. At least one of them was keeping on top of the latest social media scandals.

The grill of fencing fell, leaving a wide hole that they climbed through, still uncontested. How disheartening.

"We are wasting time," Deka groused. "There's nothing here. I can feel it."

So could Adi. The ground beneath her feet didn't vibrate with electricity. Nothing hummed at all. She should have sensed something. Anything. However, admitting that her cousin was possibly right? Not about to happen.

"It only seems like that. They've got the place heavily shielded, I'll wager."

"Of course they do," Deka said with a roll of her eyes, "because no one ever notices major construction happening in their town."

"Not if it's happening underground."

"It still requires supplies. Don't you think people would notice construction trucks and cement mixers and electricians and stuff parading in and out all the time? Not to mention, wouldn't the workers talk about it?"

Logic. Who used that as an argument? "Then how do the super villains do it? Hunh? Explain that."

Deka made a rude gesture instead. "I don't have to explain it because it's fiction. You know, as in make-believe."

"You have no imagination." Whereas Adi had too much of it. Plus, she had a healthy dose of boredom, which meant she looked for any excuse to get out. Now if only those excursions didn't result in sirens most of the time. Her sister Aimi complained that being her alibi was cutting into her alone time with her mate.

Exactly.

Duh.

The first two obstacles overcome, they ran across the barren lawn. Nothing barked. No one yelled, "Halt." Not a single bullet furrowed the hard-packed dirt. Such a letdown.

They reached the front door of the place, boarded over with *Do Not Trespass* spray-painted in large letters. All of the windows on this level sported wooden shutters. Nailed and glued. Kind of like sex sometimes.

The barrier was meant as a deterrent—to those who obeyed human laws anyway. For a dragon, it looked more like someone begging for a break-in. Adi couldn't resist. Her need to see what existed on the other side, in any situation, was why she always carried a crowbar—it would also double as a weapon in case of a zombie apocalypse. A dual-purpose tool, which increased her efficiency. *See, Mother. I didn't ignore all my lessons.*

A quick rummage through her bag brought forth her two-foot leverage. The plywood creaked and squealed as she heaved with the crowbar. Nails ripped loose, and there was a crackle as dried glue cracked. Some of it held tight, though, and the plywood snapped suddenly, sending Adi stumbling.

"Fucker." She tackled it from the other side while Deka took a selfie and loaded it to her Snapchat account.

"You'd better have gotten my good side," Adi growled as she heaved off another huge plank, revealing her prize—the glass doors into this place. Since she didn't see a lock, her crowbar acted as a key. She gave it a mighty swing and braced for the musical tinkle of breaking glass.

Bang. Bounce. She staggered from the door, arm vibrating. Not a single crack. Maybe she hadn't hit it hard enough.

Bringing back the arm holding the crowbar, Adi swung with more force.

Bang. The recoil proved worse than the first time. And still nothing. She glared at the offending glass. It mocked her with its unscratched surface.

Deka sighed. "Dude, it's like earthquake proof. And besides, why are you trying to break it? It's not locked. See?" She yanked at the portal, and it opened. "No electricity means no power to the magnetic locks. It's probably why they plywood sheeted it."

"I knew that." Adi strutted in with her chin held high. Never admit ignorance, unless the person hearing it is going to die. Deka would live another day. But the weekend was uncertain if she kept running her smart mouth.

Entering the lobby, Adi shuddered. Ugh. What a creepy location. The pristineness of the place proved spookier than any cobweb-riddled and rotted mansion.

"Damn, this place is cleaner than the house," Deka remarked.

Too clean. Adi wandered around, looking for any kind of odor that didn't have a bleached overtone. "Whatever was happening here, they didn't want anyone finding out about it. But no one is perfect. They had to have forgotten something."

"So where do you want to start looking?"

"Below ground." She stared at the shiny faux marble floor. "That's where the really interesting shit happens."

Maybe this time she would find the secret lab. Except the stairwell didn't have any stairs going down. Not even a door. None of the rooms on the main level had any kind of passage leading to a sublevel. Not even the utility room with its pipes and conduits. The giant breaker board showed the main power to the building turned off. Flicking up the main switch didn't bring anything to life.

Her lips turned down. "They cut the electricity to the place."

"Because no one is using it." Deka snapped her gum, the cherry aroma a vivid contrast to the aesthetically clean nature of the place.

"No one is using this *level*," Adi corrected. "We need to go down."

"If there is a down. We searched every inch of the main floor. Nothing."

"We didn't try the elevator."

"On account that it doesn't work so well without power."

"I'm going to look."

While Deka grumbled, she nonetheless followed, taking charge of the crowbar to pry the door to the elevator shaft open. The cab was present, and it took only a boost to go through the hatch in the ceiling. Deka quickly followed.

They sat in almost pure darkness until Adi pulled out some glow sticks from an inner pocket. She cracked one and left it atop the elevator box. She tossed the other over the side. It didn't fall far.

Don't let Deka be right. She couldn't afford to be wrong again.

She scrambled to the edge and grabbed hold

of the ladder bolted to the wall. She took it down and not very far. Maybe another ten feet below the main level where the elevator cab was stopped.

From the ladder, she jumped onto the metal plates that comprised the floor. Grimy with dust, they looked like they'd sat here forever. The green glow of her stick lit the space with the silent machines and stopped gears. She didn't see a single exit out of here other than back up the way they'd come. She peeked all over for a trap door, a conduit big enough for a body. Anything.

She was sadly disappointed.

"Now are you ready to admit defeat?" Deka asked, joining her at the bottom.

"I'm telling you, there's something here. I know it." Knew it, yet couldn't find it.

"If there was, it's gone now. We're wasting our time."

"Maybe we should check the top levels."

"For wh—"

Creak. Deka abruptly stopped talking as they both peered upward.

"What was that?" Adi whispered, although she'd seen enough movies to guess.

The elevator suspended over them jolted again, but they were already moving to flatten themselves against the wall as it plummeted down, the ten feet or so; not far, but enough to make noise—and squish them if they'd still been under it.

The sound of the crash reverberated, and she clenched her teeth, more in annoyance. "What the fuck?"

"More like who," Deka replied, peering upward. Her eyes flashed green in the dark.

"We are not alone. Halle-freaking-lujah." Adi sang the happy words. "About time someone challenged us. Let's go find them."

They dove for the ladder at the same time and hand slapped each other as they strove to choose who would climb first.

Adi won.

She clambered dragon-quick—which she might add was vastly superior to monkey-quick—and sprang onto the roof of the elevator, ready to fight.

Deka joined her a moment later.

"Do you see anyone?" her cousin asked. "Yoo-hoo. We're still here. Come and get us."

"Shh. You idiot. We don't want to scare them off." Inviting prey to their death always seemed to spook them.

"Well, I wouldn't have to if they weren't so rude in hiding themselves. I mean, really. Why go through the trouble of dropping an elevator on us if they're not going to follow through and make sure the job is done?"

A good point. "Slackers. Whoever it was must have come in through the lobby. The cut is low on the cable." She held it up and showed its clean edge.

"Which means they're not far. Wheee." Deka yodeled as she sprang for the lip of the door, now above the elevator cab.

"Save some for me," Adi hollered as she quickly followed.

She spilled out into the main lobby and found Deka standing still. Probably on account of her staring at the huge device sitting on the floor.

The one counting down. Twelve. Eleven.

"I don't remember seeing this when we came in."

Ten.

"On account it wasn't here."

Nine.

Shit. She slapped Deka in the arm.

Eight.

They pivoted, and their toes dug for purchase as they began to sprint.

Seven. Six.

The door seemed much farther away than Adi remembered.

Five. Four. Three.

The outside air hit them, but they didn't stop.

Two.

She pushed herself as hard as she could.

One.

Boom.

The explosion grabbed and tossed her, flinging her easily through the air, making her wish she had a cape.

Instinct had her grabbing for a branch instead of hitting it face first. The jolt as she halted her momentum almost ripped her arms out of their sockets.

By a stroke of mischance, Deka hit the same branch.

Crack.

The limb broke. Not entirely Adi's fault, and neither was Deka's broken leg her doing for rolling instead of providing a safety cushion for the heifer to hit.

But, apparently, that and a list of other things was the reason why there would be no more exploring empty buildings.

The crushing edict, handed down by her mother, the Sept matriarch, caused a terrible toll on her hoard—she ate until her belly bloated past the waistband of her pants. #foodbaby.

Once the sugar coma wore off, she was over her initial funk. Just because her mother forbade her didn't mean Adi would give up looking.

According to Adi's gut, Bittech was still out there, somewhere, experimenting with a dragon.

A Gold dragon. And she planned to be the one to find it and add it to her hoard. #goldisadragonsbestfriend

Chapter Two

Someone entered my room.

The lock on the door to his room didn't click or show any resistance when he turned the key. Dexter paused and stared at the knob through thick lenses. He'd left it locked, of that he was certain.

Perhaps the landlady had come to check on his unit, maybe to make a bed or change some sheets. Something he'd thus far undertaken himself. Then again, Mrs. Givry had warned him when she rented him the room that she wasn't a maid, saying, "You'll take care of yourself and your room while you're boarding here. There are cleaning supplies under the bathroom sink."

Not the most amenity-providing residence, but he held his tongue. There weren't many places left to bunk in town. Lytropia Institute had proven a boon to the small town, boosting vacancy rates to zero. With space lacking, it meant even homeowners could get in on the boom, offering spare rooms to visitors—for a premium price. But the job Dexter had plucked was so worth it.

His hand gripped the knob, and he turned it, pushing the door open, revealing bit by bit his bedroom with its three-piece attached bath, which meant privacy. Much appreciated.

What he didn't appreciate was seeing a strange woman sprawled on his bed, sifting through his comic book collection. A very unique collection that she should most definitely not touch.

"Ahem." In order to prevent screaming, he thought it best not to startle her too much. Except she didn't take note of his arrival at all.

The woman lying on her stomach on his bed, casually flipping pages, didn't even look up, just bobbed her head side to side as she read. Her short and streaked hair—pastel pieces mixed with light blonde—dangled in her face, and her legs, bent at the knees, swung back and forth, bouncing off her butt.

Absolute insouciance at its most blatant. "Who are you? What are you doing in my apartment?" he demanded. The right thing to say, but the bad boy inside took note of her skintight jeans with holes in strategic spots, like over the curve of her buttocks. The pale flesh peeked through the tear, just begging for a set of teeth marks.

Wrong thought to have right now. He averted his gaze and caught hers. The dancing light in them mocked.

"I'm the woman who's going to rock your world."

She said it so matter-of-factly. Perhaps it worked with other men. Not him.

"You are the woman who will remove herself immediately from my room."

"But if I'm gone, how are we supposed to have fun?" She presented the most perfect pout, which turned quickly into a mischievous smirk. "And I like to have *fun*."

So did he, but on his terms. "Who are you? Are you related to Mrs. Givry?"

"Related?" Gusty laughter escaped her, rich and genuine. "No more than you are. I have to say, you're not what I expected. When the landlady described you, she mentioned something about you being a big dorky fellow. But you don't look dorky at all. Smart, yes, but I like smart. She was right about your size, though. You're awfully big." Her gaze roved his entire body, starting at his face, moving down, and stopping at the spot below his belt.

Thank God for loose pants. Apparently, he was revisiting his teen years, back when a puff of wind from any direction would set his dick off.

Now imagine her blowing. He could. That was the problem. He nudged his glasses farther up the bridge of his nose. "Could you please leave before I am forced to take action?" He presented his most prim and proper appearance.

"Take action? That sounds ominously delicious." Her expression somehow managed to brighten a few more degrees. She flopped onto her back, arms akimbo, lips curved in a wide smile. "Take me, gumdrop. I'm yours."

"Gumdrop?" He couldn't help but repeat the stupid appellation.

"Well, yeah, on account I could suck on you for a long time." She winked.

He couldn't believe her temerity. His lips clamped tightly. Speaking seemed to only encourage her.

Exactly, which was why his dick thought *it* should get a chance to speak.

Hell no. "Leave now."

"No can do." She sang the words.

"Do you need help?" He'd gladly show her the door. He didn't have time to deal with this kind of madness, but at the same time, he also knew better than to put his hands on her. Today's laws really were tight about everything. Best to talk her into departing without drama.

"I already get help, thank you. Great lady, too, my head shrink. She totally gets me. She says I have rebellion issues." The woman on his bed did an all-body shrug, drawing attention to her lithe frame. "I totally want to get that tattooed on my ass. What about you? Do you have any tattoos? I have one in my tramp stamp spot. Wasn't easy to get either. My skin doesn't hold ink very well." She rolled onto her stomach again, crushing more comics under her body, especially when she wiggled to stick her bottom in the air and yanked up her shirt to show him the Chinese serpent sailing across her lower back.

A nice tattoo, but he wasn't about to encourage her with friendly chatter. His lips tightened. "You are ruining my comics."

"These"—she held up one and waved it in question—"are the most boring comics ever."

"Because a certain IQ level is required to figure them out."

The insult didn't go over her head. Her eyes widened. "Did you just call me dumb? And here I thought you were just the yummiest thing since S'mores-flavored milkshakes a minute ago. Not a smooth move, gumdrop. I'm not a person you should annoy."

"If you don't like it, leave." He wasn't usually this rude to the opposite sex, but, apparently, she brought out something special in him.

"Fine. Be that way." She rolled off his bed, moving with a fluid grace that almost hypnotized. She stopped in front of him. Close, very close.

In order to meet her gaze, he'd have to look down, way down. He knew this game, and he wasn't about to play it. He sidestepped the stranger, putting his back to the wall and extending his arm to indicate the open door. "Have a good evening."

She grinned. "Oh, I will. And feel free to barge in if you hear screaming. It doesn't take me long to get ready for round two."

It took a few blinks and a moment spent not breathing to grasp what she meant. Her sashay across the hall to the other door, and the wink over her shoulder as she slid into the room opposite his, sealed the deal.

The lunatic is staying here, too.

He found the thought disturbingly titillating. But he had work to do.

So the radio went on, lest he be tempted to listen, the firewalls and redirects went into play, and he spent some time searching for patterns and keys in chunks of code. Fun times. Usually. So why did he find himself staring at the door every so often? It didn't help that his mind proved to have x-ray vision. His vivid imagination saw across the hall, imagined the hot chick lying on the bed, lean legs spread, pinkness showing, her fingers working.

It took a cold shower and some finger work of his own to deal with his problem. Even then, as he left his room, Dex couldn't help but stare at the door across from his and wonder what she did behind it. *Does she need a hand? Or a tongue…*

No.

What I need is a fucking beer.

Chapter Three

I should have bought some beer.

Parched. Dying. Adi was so thirsty, and this room didn't have a mini-fridge or a bar. Not even a single pint-sized alcoholic treat. It didn't have much except for the basics—a double-sized bed, a battered nightstand, and a chest of drawers. Old, yet solidly built wooden furniture.

The kind that snaps and crackles when it burns. She did so love watching the flames, especially when she had some marshmallows on hand.

But she wasn't here to cause fires—yet—and the room, while small, would only be temporary. So she made the most of it.

Adi danced around the bedroom, the cramped space meaning she used the bed as part of her dance floor. As the tunes rocked and rolled, providing a hum that would be hard to penetrate, she made some calls via the headset she wore.

The line rang. Clicked. Rang again. Clicked again, running through several layers of security to ensure she couldn't be traced. When someone answered, "What do you want?" Adi uttered a lowly spoken, "The condor has landed."

Her sister on the other end of the call sighed. "Don't start with that again. You know I hate the code names."

"Not my fault you got stuck with cuckoo." Actually, it was Adi's fault Aimi had drawn that bird name because she had rigged the whole draw with her cousins and aunts. Some people were still complaining about the mission names they'd gotten. As if there was something wrong with dodo and turkey.

"I don't see why you couldn't let me use eagle. No one else has it."

"It wasn't part of the pool of names when you chose."

"On purpose."

"Maybe," Adi teased.

"I wish I was an only child."

"Love you, too, sis." Aimi was her sister, twin to be exact. Not identical by any means, though. They might have shared a womb, but when it came to temperament, they differed vastly.

"If you loved me, you'd change my name to eagle."

"Can't. It's been taken."

"Since when?"

"Since you got mated and your hunk of burning love needed a name."

She could almost picture the indignant look on her sister's face. Then Adi paid for it as Aimi purred. "I think I feel an urge for some Twinkies."

"Don't you dare touch my stash of treats," Adi hissed in the microphone. The very thought of someone stealing from her hoard made her see red. *I've got a razor, and I'm not afraid to scalp her.*

"You want to save your stash of goodies, then let it be known my new code name is the swan."

"Fine." A word bitten off, but at least her hoard was safe. *My sugar. My yummy, yummy sugar.*

"Since we're on the topic of names, have you thought of one for the kid you're about to be carrying?" Aimi didn't mess around.

Adi stopped spinning and scowled, even if no one could see her. "That isn't even funny."

A loud sigh replied. "No. It's not. But your time is running out."

"I know." Not much freedom left before Adi did her duty to the family. Having a kid? Not the worst thing in the world. Grounded for nine months? Ugh. That would blow, especially since afterwards, she would only be let out to play if the matriarch of the Sept allowed it. Such was the plight of unmated dragons when they reached twenty-eight and were declared spinsters. They became the family defenders and baby makers—and not babies made the good, old-fashioned, fun way. Artificially inseminated by some kind of milkshake. No daddy took credit, although sometimes, a person could guess, and whoever kept track of these things always knew when to step in and stop a mating between couples.

No three-eyed babies with tails anymore.

Keep the blood strong. The reason they all abided by the archaic laws.

It wasn't all bad. At least her mother kept the kitchen of their house—think a modest twenty-six bedroom house—very well stocked.

"Wouldn't it be funny if I got pregnant before you?" Adi's lips turned down at her own poor joke.

"Good luck with that. Brand keeps me busy. Very busy."

For once, her sister had tossed the dirty innuendo first, which totally shocked Adi and pulled a chuckle from her. "I have to say, he's a wonderfully bad influence on you."

"So bad." Aimi purred. "So tell me about the geek. Was he as cute in person as the pictures?"

Ah, yes, her unsuspecting target. "Even cuter." The smell of him divine. An unexpected bonus. It seemed her chosen target would be more fun than expected.

Despite her mother trying to ban her from scouting out any more Bittech locations, Adi couldn't sit still. Since the known Bittech locations proved a bust, she'd gone looking for new targets.

Still active targets.

When a business shut down, under shady circumstances, it wasn't unusual for a new business to spring up, pretending to be unrelated. But Adi had a hunch about Lytropia, so she'd cased the institute. She'd dug up every bit of information she could on the seemingly benign medical research facility that operated on the outskirts of Idontgiveafuck. Closely related to Fuckinghole and Boredomkills. Adi preferred to play in the city, but in this case, she'd made an exception to go where the action was.

Before she'd descended on the town and graced them with her glory, hours had been spent perusing pictures and employee dossiers, especially those for the peeps commuting in and out of the institute each day. She pored over online presences, looking for potential breaches. She studied the digital footprint of every person going in and out of the LI building, looking for just the right target—*my way in*.

Adi settled on Dexter… Mostly on account of his big glasses and shitty haircut; he made her think of a certain geeky hero in disguise. Just in case he was undercover, she'd searched his room thoroughly when she arrived. It proved disappointingly empty of cape and tights.

Wonder if he'd wear an outfit if one were custom-made for him? She knew a seamstress who could do great—and at times, obscene—things with Lycra.

Further searching of Dexter's room had shown he didn't have any lube, handcuffs, or dildos either. But he did have condoms, so he wasn't a complete prude.

Her sister laughed in her ear. "Day one, and you already made contact. Way to go. Did you guys hit it off?"

"In a sense." He definitely might have wanted to hit her. Mr. Sexy-In-Glasses certainly didn't seem awed by the hot girl in his room. #thatneverhappened. Didn't he know how it was supposed to work? Dorky tech guys always wanted to bone the hot techy girl.

Except Dexter didn't know Adi was a geek like him. A cool geek, of course. Hello. Look at her, totally cute. A boy like him should have been drooling all over her.

Worssship isss good. Her inner dragon ever did have a lisp. Drove Mother wild.

"When are you going to see the geek again?"

If he had a choice? Probably never. "We haven't quite nailed that down. But it won't be tonight. Tonight I'm going to soak in the local ambiance."

"You mean get drunk at the local bar?"

Her sister knew her well. "Best place for gossip in town."

"Just be careful. You don't exactly blend in."

"Of course I don't. You can't dumb down brilliance." Modesty, a thing only humans aspired to.

"Keep me updated on things in town."

"I will if you do the same for at home. What did Mom say after she found out I left?" Adi had left without permission because she knew what her mother would have said if she'd asked. "Did she like totally freak?"

"Actually, she didn't. Apparently, Aunt Waida is somewhere in town, too, so you might be on to something."

"Aha. I knew it." And yes, this was totally different from the other times Adi thought she'd known it and had been wrong. Totally different.

"Good news is, you can call on her if you run into trouble."

"Call on Auntie? Do you hate me that much?" With Aunt Waida, one never knew what would happen. Things sometimes blew up. Or disappeared, silently. Other times, there was running while screaming about demons involved.

Auntie tended to add interesting outcomes to the mix. *Maybe I should give her a shout.*

Later, though. First, Adi needed to scope out the town and the residents. And while her choice—a bar—did serve beer, it wasn't her primary reason for going.

Snicker.

Okay, so it was, but in her defense, she was thirsty.

Upon walking into the raucous bar with its stripped wooden plank floors, open beam ceiling, and jean-clad clientele, she knew exactly what to do to get the crowd giving her what she needed—free beer.

Yeehaw.

Chapter Four

"Yeehaw!"

More than one voice shouted it, and it didn't take long to see why. Dexter couldn't help but notice the action the moment he walked into the bar.

Not her again. It seemed he was doomed to run into his new neighbor across the hall today.

The short-haired pixie rode the mechanical bull on the far side of the bar like they were fused together, her thighs clamped tightly around the barrel shape, her upper body thrusting in time with the bucking metal beast.

She held on with only one hand while the other waved. Through all the humping and bumping, she laughed and yodeled. Someone was having entirely too much fun—and provoking very naughty ideas.

Men surrounded her, lots of men, their gazes drawn to her, magnetized by her vibrant nature. How could they not find themselves drawn? She evoked pure carnal delight.

She also posed a distraction. *Look away.* Now wasn't the time to ogle her ridiculously firm grip or her thrusting breasts. He had more important things to do than lust after the girl—with a bed across the hall from his. He'd chosen this bar so he could relax with a beer while catching up with someone.

Catching sight of a familiar face, he weaved past tables, avoiding the dance floor and moving away from the side of the room with the bucking bull—and she whom he would not think of. He slid into a booth at the back, the burgundy-colored leather scratched, faded, and, in some places, torn. Duct tape mended other injuries to the banquette. The seat didn't have any padding, the surface unforgiving to his ass. No getting too comfortable here.

The table was bolted to the floor, a wise move by any establishment that encouraged the ingestion of copious amounts of alcohol. Hot heads always seemed to get fierier after a few brews, which was why he tended to pace himself when he did drink. Not because he fought, but because he liked to be able to dodge if needed.

He avoided the sticky spot on the lacquered, wooden surface as he took a spot across from the guy already nursing a brown bottle of beer.

Slouched as he was, a person could not tell Calvin stood over six-foot-five, but the width of his shoulders would still cause pause. He was big. Stupid big. And, thankfully, a friend.

Good, because Dex didn't want to be his enemy. Dexter had seen a man get clocked by Calvin's unyielding fist. That stupid bastard had sucked his meals through a straw for months.

"Nice seeing you again. It's been a while." Dexter inclined his head. His friend looked well, his pate shaven close to the scalp, his shirt collared and clean, his eyes clear. No warning signs of impending madness. But the night was young.

Calvin rolled his shoulders, an earthquake in motion. "I've been busy."

"I know the feeling." And that was all that had to be said because, with good friendships, time apart didn't matter. Coming together even for a short moment was as familiar as pulling on a well-worn pair of jeans. He gestured to the beer. "I see you got a head start on me."

"I had to. I got here early and enjoyed a few pounds of wings. I would have saved you some but"—Calvin grinned—"they were really good. What took you so long to get here?"

"I'm one minute early," he retorted.

"Exactly. You used to arrive fifteen before the time. What gives? You getting slow with old age?"

"Decrepit. Bought myself a walker just last week. I'm getting the bars for the shower in a few days."

"Don't worry. I'll shoot you before you get to the point you're wearing a diaper and gumming your food."

Dexter couldn't help a snort of amusement. "And that's what makes you a true friend."

A waitress walked by, and Dex lifted two fingers. She acknowledged with a nod before she bobbed off through the crowd, her rounded ass cheeks peeking past her short jeans skirt. Cute, but not as cute as the girl currently dismounting the bull on the far side of the room amidst whistles and cheers.

Pixie-girl garnered way too much attention

with her laughing and smiling, and hey, was that dude trying to grab her ass?

Not anymore. The groper now held his hand and glared accusingly at another man.

"You should think of taking an assistant."

The remark drew Dexter's attention back. "An assistant for what? I can handle the job just fine on my own." Computers, and especially servers, were finicky creatures. Especially networks created by someone else. Each IT guy had his own method and protections to keep his virtual space safe.

Recently hired by Lytropia Institute after their previous head tech had gone home suddenly—who would text a man pictures of his girlfriend cheating back home and then include plane tickets?—Dexter now controlled the LI network. But he'd yet to discover all the very cool nooks and crannies. He rolled his shoulders at Calvin. "I'm fine, really. Still getting my feet under me."

"If you say so."

"I do say so. So, hey, did you happen to bring any of that jam your mom is famous for?"

"Nope. I only have a jar for me. And I am not sharing. I got business in the big city, and I don't know how long it will take to handle."

"I thought you were on sabbatical."

"I was, but this job came in, and I couldn't say no. Which kind of sucks. I finally bought a place in some up-and-coming neighborhood, but because of this stupid job, I'm commuting all the fucking time."

"Is the place worth it?"

"It will be. Right now, the house is a little rough. But I've got some ideas for it."

"You're going to renovate?" Dexter snickered. "Never thought I'd see the day you'd get domesticated."

"Whoa. Slow the fuck down." Calvin appeared mildly horrified. "Never said anything about getting serious. You know I can't do that with my job. But I thought it was time I had some roots. A place to call my own and to store my toys."

Now there was something he understood. "I know that feeling." His mother's basement, while nicely appointed sometimes, did prove cloying. But she made a mean peach cobbler and apple pie, and she kept the place ready for his return in between contracts.

The beers arrived, at last, and Dexter took a long sip. Icy-cold perfection.

Calvin leaned forward. "So while I have you here, I know a guy who is looking for a whole-home, integrated security system. Whole nine yards. He's as paranoid as they come, and wants something sophisticated that he can control from his phone. You got time for it?"

"Depends on when the guy wants me to start. I'm two months in on a contract that says six."

"Too long. He's going to want someone sooner."

"Then no can do. I gotta finish this place first."

"You're nuts to be working here. Hope the money is good because it has got to be costing you a fortune in rent. I hear the town is crazy booked."

"It's a little pricy." Especially considering he was sleeping in the landlady's eldest son's room. He didn't visit anymore on account of his wife and Mrs. Givry not getting along. Imagine that. "I managed to find a place, but I've had to eat out every night, and the pickings are limited." But the lemon meringue pie was quite good. "Good thing the institute has a small cafeteria, or I'd starve for lunch." Even better, the food wasn't half bad, even if it did seem to contain more meat dishes than today's healthy society usually dictated.

Calvin snapped his fingers. "You know what, while I don't have any jam for you, I do have those golf clubs I borrowed. They're in my trunk."

"Really?" His expression brightened. "I might have a use for those. You can chuck them in my car before you leave. It's unlocked." Because who would steal it? Sometimes older was better.

"You still driving that piece of shit?"

"That 'piece of shit' has the cheapest insurance, excellent mileage, and has paid for itself ten times over." A 1980s Plymouth with a dependable engine, four doors, a boring navy blue exterior, and not even one spot of rust. He kept a strict maintenance schedule to prevent any kind of decomposition.

A grimace pulled at Calvin's features. "Anyone ever tell you that you're way too responsible?"

"You make that sound like an insult, and yet you wait until you're old and living off a government check. You'll wish you'd saved a bit during your grasshopper years and put away some money in a steady retirement plan."

"Hey, I bought a house. That counts."

"It's a start. But I'm going to wager you're driving something that cost almost as much as your house."

Calvin grinned. "The house cost more, but not by much. I won't lie, though. My little red coupe wasn't cheap. You also can't beat the features."

"Does it blow you?"

"Almost. It certainly removes panties."

Being men, this type of statement meant they clinked their beers, and they spent a half-hour more chatting before Calvin rose from the booth, his giant body unfolding. "I'd better get going before I'm too drunk to drive to the next motel. This whole town is packed."

"LI has been a boon to the local economy." If only they were as good as they seemed. The perfect veneer hid a dark truth.

"Good luck on the job. Don't be afraid to drop me a line if you want to get together again. I won't be too far."

"I will." They didn't hug or do anything emasculating. Just two friends getting together for a drink because they happened to cross paths. But never doubt they'd drop everything to go to the other's aid. They had the academy to thank for that.

With his friend gone, that didn't mean Dexter quickly followed. He'd long ago developed a tolerance and responsibility when it came to booze. He remembered what his mother had gone through. *What I went through.* He'd never be the man his father was.

Never. He'd kill himself first.

Spotting his waitress, he ordered another beer. It arrived in a sweaty flounce, his neighbor across the hall intercepting the waitress and swiping the bottle off her tray.

Pixie-girl slid into the seat across from him and then, instead of handing the bottle over, took the first crisp sip. "Aah. That's some good stuff," she exclaimed.

"You stole my beer."

"Finders. Keepers."

"You didn't find it. You stole it from the waitress."

"I did not steal it. I told her to put it on your tab."

"What makes you think I have a tab?"

"Because you didn't give her anything when she delivered the last two."

The shrewd observation took him by surprise.

She took a sip. "Mmm. That really *is* some good stuff."

"I wouldn't know," was his dry reply.

"Want to share?" She took another swig before handing him the bottle, her pink gloss marring the rim.

It occurred to him to refuse. To tell her to keep it, but judging by the glint in her eye, she expected it. He wouldn't let her win. "Thanks." He grabbed the cool glass and placed his mouth on the rim, right over where she'd touched. He tasted peaches and cream before the bitterness of the brew eradicated it.

"So, what's a stuck-up guy like you doing in a place like this?" she asked, leaning forward and putting her chin in her hands. "I thought you were going to bed. I even pictured you there. Naked." Wink.

Funny, he'd done the same thing. With her, not him. "I was meeting a friend passing through."

"The good-looking fellow? I can see why you're interested."

It took him a moment to grasp her implication. "You think—no, we're not friends like that. We're just old buddies. From school."

"So you date…"

"Women. I'm into women." He almost growled the words.

"How deep into?"

"How what?"

"Deep? Into a woman? As in six inches, eight, get-the-lube size?" An eyebrow lifted as she asked, completely serious, while he was probably, for the first time, completely flustered by a woman.

"We are not having this conversation."

"Shy? Or don't you know? I thought all guys measured it."

"Not all guys." Although, he could guesstimate.

"If you'd prefer, you could give me a demonstration of its length."

Madness was being tempted to. "This is hardly the time or place, don't you think?"

"A shy guy. I can dig that. We'll go somewhere else then. A place with a door. Bathroom stall work?"

"No!"

"You are a prude. Well, just our luck it doesn't matter if I say your place or mine, they're the same distance." She smiled as she tried to trap him.

"The landlady's rules state no fornicating under her roof." She'd waxed quite vehemently about the sin of fornicating outside of marriage. It was why she no longer talked to a pair of her daughters. The whore of Babylon had nothing on them, apparently.

"Worried about Mrs. G? Bah. She'll be in bed, probably snoring. We'll just have to be quiet. We can use my panties as a gag."

"No."

"You're not a screamer? Disappointing. But I'll get over it. So, whose place you want to hit? I think we should go with mine since my bed doesn't squeak much."

"We are not having sex." Which, said out loud, sounded really dumb. What man in his right mind wouldn't want to have sex with her? She was utterly adorable with her streaked hair, teased in all directions, her eyes dark with eyeliner and mascara, her lips luscious and tempting.

"Again with that nasty use of the word no. I don't get it. Are you saving yourself for marriage? I can respect that. We can always just indulge in oral instead."

Thank God for loose pants and a table. This woman had the ability to throw him. What he didn't understand was his attraction. While cute as a button, she also sported a nose ring, several ear piercings, and a punk-girl look that involved bright colors in layers and rips.

He usually preferred his lady friends in business suits with hair neatly pinned and in need of mussing. He also usually didn't have to deal with blatant sexual proposition.

"Are you always this forward when it comes to guys and sex?"

She leaned forward. "Usually, I only have to look at a fellow, and he's ready to drop his pants." Her lips curved. "You're making me work for it. I like it."

Then his plan was backfiring because she wasn't supposed to like anything about him. He couldn't get involved with anyone right now, especially not this brazen woman. Time to call it a night. "Why don't you have the rest?" He slid the beer bottle across the table and stood. Thinking about his mother helped him to not suffer embarrassment.

Embarrassment didn't seem to be something she suffered from. She hopped up. "Oh, don't leave on account of me."

"I wasn't. I have to work in the morning."

"Me too."

"Doing what?"

"Nails." She flashed her fingers, the nails on them short and clean. "Not mine, but other people's, of course. I'm a nail artist."

"There's such a thing?"

"Did you just diss me?" Her eyes widened. "Naughty, gumdrop. You are so asking for an angry mauling."

He wasn't quite sure what that meant, but more disturbing, he almost asked her to demonstrate. Instead, he moved past her with a muttered, "Good night."

However, it wasn't a good night, not when

he spent a few hours lying in his bed, listening for her to come back to the boarding house. Then more time spent wondering who she did go home with.

The alarm went off much too early, and he glared at her door on his way downstairs.

I don't care what she did last night. Or who.

Not one fucking bit.

Chapter Five

Fucking sunlight.

Dawn crept with disturbing brightness over the horizon. Having partied to the closing of the bar, Adi would have liked a few more hours of sleep. At least she wasn't hungover. Alone in a strange town wasn't the place to find out if a drunk girl was safe from the populace—and a dragon safe from a certain institute.

Nothing worse than waking up strapped to a table with tubes poking through your skin. Or so Aunt Juanita claimed. She never was the same after her supposed alien abduction. Adi's mother claimed it was more likely a case of 'shrooms.

As Adi showered and brushed her teeth, she checked in on a few things. Mainly, the man across the hall.

The bug she'd planted indicated that her target had gone to his room the previous night and remained there. Even once he'd left the bar, she'd kept dibs via an app on her phone—an app she designed, hold the applause.

Today, the plan was to bug him a little more, starting with his car. The tiny tracker went under the front passenger seat. A very unimpressive seat, she might add.

The vehicle might appear super clean, but it was also the epitome of old and boring. This wasn't some kind of muscle car from the sixties or a sweet, fast ride from the eighties. He drove a dependable, boring, no-bells-and-whistles car.

A vintage car from the eighties no less. So she took a selfie and posted it. #drivinginaclassic.

As she waited for it to go viral—or at least get one like from her sister—she sipped coffee from an old and chipped mug. The old biddy renting out rooms in her house let her have it for a price, a steep fee that Adi would be invoicing her mother for. *Don't work for free.* A dragon family motto.

The driver-side door to the car opened, and her adorable, geeky target stuck his head inside. "What the hell are you doing?" he asked, his astonished expression made owlish by his glasses.

"Waiting for you. Naughty boy, making me wait. You're really going to have to hustle if you're going to drop me off at the salon and still make it to work on time." Stupid airport wouldn't let her rent a car without a license. Why rent, though, when it was so much better to carpool? Especially when the chauffeur was cute.

"I won't need to hurry because I'm not dropping you off anywhere." He stated it quite firmly.

So cute. As if he'd win. "You are dropping me off, gumdrop, and the longer you argue about it, the later it gets. So get your sweet cheeks into that driver's seat. Or would you prefer I took the wheel? They revoked my license a while back, something about being a menace to society. Overblown, if you ask me. And I wouldn't have hit anything if that third cop car hadn't cut me off." She flexed her fingers. "Don't worry, though. I'm sure I haven't lost the knack. They say driving is like riding a bike. Don't hit the trees. Because then insurance companies get involved, and things get complicated."

Sigh. A loud sigh. The kind of sigh Adi often heard from her mother, but she never wanted to plant a wet kiss on her mama's lips.

Dexter, on the other hand, looks tastier than a Twinkie.

He'd look even better in the hoard. Splayed naked on her treasure pile, gooey cake and icing smearing his body and requiring a lick.

Mmm. Licking.

Down, dragon, she cautioned her inner beast as Dexter slid into the driver's seat and started the engine. For its age, it ran rather smoothly. Actually, the entire car was clean and well kept. Just old, as in roll down the windows with a crank old. And who the hell still had vinyl seats?

Bet these are killer in the sun. "Thanks for the ride."

"As if I had a choice."

"You have the option of doing it my way or arguing for a while and still doing it my way." Because hers was the only way. Aimi often declared the world revolved around her. Adi begged to differ.

"Are your lack of listening skills and manners because you were raised by wolves?" he asked as he pulled out of the rooming house driveway.

"Most people liken my mother to a dragon."

"A tough lady?"

"You have no idea." Her mother held the title of the toughest matriarch in all the Septs. Adi wasn't ever able to see her mother fight in a true battle situation, but she'd seen the mad respect her mom got from the other dragons, and the envious hate. Only the great inspired that.

She'd grown up hearing the stories. Aunt Waida even had a scar and often pointed to it with an ominously declared, "No one touches the last piece of your great-grandma's Black Forest cake, not when Zahra is around."

"Does your mother know you accost men in their rooms?" Dexter wouldn't look at her as he drove the speed limit along the country road that led into town.

"Who do you think taught me?" She grinned. "Lighten up, gumdrop. It wasn't that big of a deal. The landlady happened to mention you, so I wanted to say hi."

"Only hi? Then why is it that I'm driving you to work?"

"Save the planet. Haven't you heard of sharing a commute to lessen the impact on the environment when it comes to the burning of fossil fuels?"

"That has to be the most intelligent bullshit you've spouted so far."

"I'm just full of surprises. You'll see."

"Doubtful, since we won't be seeing each other again. Tomorrow, you will find another method of transportation."

"You are so entertaining. I can see we shall

have tons of fun."

"Exactly where downtown are you working?" He bit out the words, and she saw him gripping the wheel oh so tightly. The dear man was very agitated. But interested.

A woman could tell. What she understood less was her determination to win him over.

Adi explained where to find the nail salon, and within ten minutes, he'd arrived, the main street bereft of traffic at this time of morning, most shops only starting to open for business. She hopped out, but before shutting the passenger door, she leaned in and announced quite brightly, "See you at five when you pick me up."

She loved the way his mouth rounded, and she skipped off before he'd finished saying "no."

Nasty word, and since she refused to acknowledge it for her mother, she certainly wouldn't pay it any mind coming from him.

Although her teasing of the poor man did, however, remind her of a lesson from Aunt Yolanda. "Don't play with the humans. Until you're ready to eat them. They're easily traumatized, which sours the meat." They also bruised like peaches. It was why she wasn't allowed to play dodgeball once she hit puberty.

Cry babies.

Dexter left, his car smoothly pulling away without a single screech of tires. Very unlike her family, who sometimes had contests on longest rubber streaks.

Even more astonishing, she realized he'd still not asked her name. *Probably because he doesn't need it since he's got a super cute nickname for me.* She couldn't wait to hear it.

She flounced into the shop, her first day of work replacing the pregnant girl who had the nerve to deliver early—at least according to the owner, Sally, who'd lamented, "And she couldn't have chosen a worse time. We've been super busy here ever since LI opened. Between the doctors and scientists working over there and the press"—a press curious about the shifters LI was studying for the public—"we've got more appointments than we can handle." Which made it easy for an outsider to apply and get the position of nail artist.

Because what better place for gossip was there than a local hair and nail salon? She spent her entire day listening and slyly asking questions because she could only learn so much online.

"I hear all the guards are shifter fellows. Barney says they're not allowed to come into town on account they can't control themselves around the ladies, especially if they get drunk." Titter.

"Is it true their things," said the woman with a purple-hued bouffant and a coy smile, "are barbed at the end?"

"I hear they're all hung like stallions."

"Size is all well and good, but do they know how to use it?"

But the biggest question of all that fluttered in the air, unspoken but thought—could humans become Lycans or shapeshifters, too? The very idea of it frightened the humans.

Such a groundless fear. Shapeshifting was not a disease or a virus, but the rumors persisted since the shapeshifters of the world had come out of the closet.

Parker's fault. A wolf with delusions of grandeur, he'd outed almost every hidden creature in the world with no mind to the chaos and strife it might cause the humans. The humans who couldn't help but bleat in fear.

Baaaaa.

What did Mother say about us calling them that?

It was actually Aunt Yolanda who'd said to never refer to the humans as sheep. They were not to be preyed upon. Which contradicted Aunt Waida, who usually added, "Unless they threaten us." Then bring on the mint jelly for dipping.

Although, with Dexter, she thought he'd taste yummier smeared in icing. Drool.

"New girl, get to work."

The snapping fingers almost got torn off, but since that might make her stay uncomfortable, Adi refrained and instead—ugh—worked.

A variety of customers spent the day revolving in and out of the shop. They chattered as they received treatment. Many spoke about the shifters—and were laughably misinformed.

"I hear if you sleep with a werewolf on a full moon you'll have puppies."

And Canadians lived in igloos year round.

Useless info. The entire day went along that vein, lots of speculation but very little actual gossip about LI itself. None of her clients that day worked there directly, but she didn't get discouraged. Even girl scientists and doctors liked to look their best, and this was the only true place in town to go. And it was proving a bust so far.

So much for her hunch. Bittech was gone, and there was nothing to indicate that this new company had anything to do with them. On the outside, they seemed on the up and up.

I think that's a façade. Gut instinct said this place was up to no good, but before she called the wrath of dragon Septs down on it, she had to be sure. *I need evidence.*

Spoilsports with their fact-checking, wanting the t's crossed and i's dotted. Back in the day, as her mother would say, they'd just swoop in and raze the place to the ground. But that was in a time when dragons still ruled the skies and were considered the ultimate predator.

As it turned out, humans, with their cunning and weapons, proved deadliest of all. They had just about culled the dragons into extinction. It had taken centuries to rebuild, and centuries to perfect the art of hiding in plain sight.

Look at me, mixing with the common folk. They don't even know there's a princess in their midst.

Stupid peasants should be bowing.

"Hey, new girl, stop mooning about and grab a broom."

Showing more restraint than her family would, Adi grabbed a long-handled broom instead of a sword.

Off with their heads wasn't a game she could play today.

But maybe soon…#lifegoals

Chapter Six

What am I doing here? At exactly four fifty-nine p.m., waiting a few storefronts down from the salon, Dexter lay his head down on the steering wheel, not quite banging it but close.

Pixie-girl was probably kidding when she'd said she expected him. But what if she wasn't? What if, at five o'clock, she stood outside, waiting and waiting for a ride that never came?

Why do I even care?

He shouldn't.

This was pathetic.

Five o'clock came.

He really should get going.

Five after.

Maybe his clock ran fast. Nope. His watch, which ran off the web, showed the same time as his car.

Ten minutes. He was calling himself stupid and turning the key to start the car when he saw her sauntering out.

She emerged and took a deep breath, her face tilted to the sky and the waning sunlight, the days shortening as fall took hold of the land. Her mop of hair looked as rumpled as ever.

Breath taken, she pivoted and, without

hesitation, walked toward him as if she knew exactly where he'd be.

Drive away.

Go.

Now.

He didn't move.

Her lips tilted into a smirk while her slim hips undulated in a way that drew attention to her navel and the jewel glinting in it. She slid into the passenger seat with a sparkle in her eyes that made them seem green, not brown like he'd originally thought. "Honey, I'm home. Actually, that's not accurate. If I were home, I'd be wearing a heck of a lot less clothing. I mean bras, seriously? Who intentionally wears those all day long?" Spoken and acted upon, the lacy, pink confection somehow found its way out from underneath her shirt and ended up in his backseat. It meant her cropped silk top clung to pert nipples.

He averted his gaze. "You probably should have kept that on." His hands were also glad to offer support.

"On? Whatever for? It was stifling my *creativity.*" She peeked down at her bosom.

"But we're going somewhere."

"We are? Ooh. That sounds promising. Should I remove more clothing so I'm ready?"

The car didn't waver, but something in him did. "No. I mean. No." He clenched the wheel tightly. "I mean you should stay dressed because I doubt they'll let you in for dinner if you're not fully clothed."

"Then we need a new place for dinner. I'm hungry and not in a mood to put that devilish contraption back on."

"And this is my problem how?"

"You mentioned food. And my tummy is rumbly. As in hashtag feed-me-now."

"Are you always so demanding?"

"Yes. It's one of my most endearing qualities."

"And what's your worst?" he asked without even thinking.

"My fascination with you."

"How is that bad?" He couldn't help but cast her a glance, wondering if her answer was just more smoke and mirrors, meant to throw him off.

"I'm here to do a job and show my mother I'm not a fuckup. She thinks I'm impetuous."

"You are."

"See, when you say it, it makes me sound fun. When she says it, it usually results in my getting grounded."

"You live with your mother?"

"Yes." Said with a drop of her chin and crossing of her arms. "On account that I'm not married."

For some reason, he felt a reason to divulge. "I'm not judging, just so you know. I also live with my mom."

She cast him a glance. "Why am I not surprised? Childhood bedroom or the basement?" A grin tugged at her lips. "I'm going to guess basement."

"It is. Converted into a full apartment, I might add. With a walkout so it's nice and bright."

"Basement dweller." Coughed into her hand but quite distinct.

For some reason, he found that funny and chuckled. "I guess you could say so."

"So what are we having for dinner? All this foreplay is making me hungry. And we'll need our strength for later."

He didn't bother correcting her. It was a waste of breath. "About the only place you might pass muster is the food truck in the parking lot of that big box hardware store by the highway."

She clapped her hands. "Cheeseburger, greasy fries, and onion rings. Yes! Way to sweep a girl off her feet, gumdrop. How did you know that's my favorite meal?"

He didn't. There were lots of things he didn't know about his passenger, starting with her name. "Do you know, we've yet to introduce ourselves? My name is Dexter."

"As in Dexter Morgan, that wickedly warped and yet sexy serial killer on HBO?"

"No, as in Dexter Kenneth Cline. IT specialist."

"A techy guy?" She grabbed at her heart. "Say it ain't so. Do you have any idea just how hot your geeky ass got? The only thing sexier would have been video game programmer."

At that, he couldn't help but grin a little. "In my college days, I might have dabbled and made a few apps that were just plain fun." One of which got him kicked out of college due to its R-rated nature. But even without finishing college and getting his diploma, he'd gotten noticed and headhunted. Now he worked as a freelancer, picking and choosing contracts. Never staying in one place for too long. Boredom was his enemy.

"You are all kinds of surprising, gumdrop."

"Could you try and call me Dex? The whole gumdrop thing makes me think of my grandmother and her love of hard lemon candies."

For some reason, she thought that uproariously funny. She giggled and giggled and, in panting bursts, managed a chortled, "I remind you of your grandma. Fucking priceless. Fair enough. I'll try and restrain myself."

"Thank you. And what should I call you?"

"My birth certificate says Adrienne, but my friends call me Adi. My mother calls me 'she-demon sent to trouble her,' but that's only on account of me being so special to her."

"Sounds like an interesting"—ready for the loony bin—"family."

"Totally. Wait until you meet them."

"Not likely," he muttered.

She heard him. "Never dare a Silvergrace, Dex baby. We hate to lose." She offered him a wink as she slinked out of the car, her grace sinuous in nature and attention-grabbing.

He couldn't help but stare at her ass as she walked over to the food truck and perused the menu.

Only one thing I'd like to eat. And depending on how things went with dinner, he might have his chance.

He snuck up behind Adi, but she didn't need to turn her head to know. She addressed him and not the guy taking orders from the truck. "I'll have a fully loaded cheeseburger, steamed dog with mustard, mayo, cheese, and a slice of bacon, a fry, and an onion ring with a cream soda to drink."

"And you're telling me because?"

"I'm hungry."

"And?"

"And you're wasting time. I'm fading here, can't you tell? I'll find us a table while you get me sustenance. Stat."

Off she went, leaving him to order and pay, imperious in her demands. But then again, her methods got results since he made two trips to bring them the many dishes.

He then got to watch this tiny woman demolish enough food for a few grown men, including part of his meal. When done, she popped the top button on her jeans and patted her belly. "We can now update our hashtag to food-baby-heaven."

Heaven? More like hell. He almost dove over the table. He wanted this uninhibited woman with a fervency that took him by storm. Everything about her drew him on a carnal level. She utterly fascinated him. Then he reminded himself she wasn't who she seemed.

"What's your interest in Lytropia Institute?" Without warning, he tossed the question at her and watched for her reaction.

Boredom with a hint of don't-care attitude. She shrugged. "What makes you think I have any?"

"Because they have a file on you."

"They do?" Her eyes brightened. "What does it say?"

"Plenty."

"Show me."

Since he knew how easily a phone could be hacked—he'd hacked plenty in his time—he pulled the evidence from his back pocket, unfolding the square of paper until he could slap it down on the picnic table.

"This is it? One page?" She sounded deflated. "I should have merited at least a three-page report. Hashtag disappointed."

"It says you are some kind of rich girl activist." Not just a bubbly-headed, punk-girl temptation that spelled trouble. Apparently, he wasn't the only one with secrets. It should have made him pull away from her. Instead, she just got hotter.

Hot enough to burn. But what a way to die.

Chapter Seven

Damn, I look hot.

Modesty belonged to those who lacked an awesome factor.

Adi lifted the sheet Dex had pulled out of his pocket and scanned it. The grainy, black and white image was of her, taken while riding the bull in the bar last night, meant she'd hit someone's radar. Good. She wasn't trying to be subtle.

"Where did you get this?" she asked, noticing they'd identified her in the report. Adrienne Silvergrace, and included her date of birth, along with other vital statistics, including height and weight, which was generously low.

"I got it from my work at the institute."

"You work in that big old medical lab place?" She batted her lashes. "How fascinating. Tell me more."

"You do realize that doesn't work in real life."

"You're right. I should have led with more cleavage first." Problem was, she'd removed her bra, and if she took off her shirt, too, then who knew what would happen. The judge had warned her against doing that in public again, lest she cause an even bigger car pileup.

He yanked the report back and stabbed at some writing. "According to this, you're not really a nail artist."

"I could be. I'm good at it. But I tend to not keep jobs long. I have issues with authority."

"Do you also have issues with companies like LI?"

"What do you mean?"

"Why the interest in LI? What do you know about them?"

"I know what everyone knows, that they are running tests on shapeshifters in order to give answers to the populace. Should they be spayed or neutered? Do they require a muzzle at work? Can so-and-so Joe werewolf at work give his case of the fleas to his human co-workers?"

"I think their purpose is a little more serious than that."

"Of course it is. They're looking to prove that shapeshifters pose no threat to mankind." They didn't, but dragons most certainly did. "And to do so, they're testing live subjects."

"Perfectly legal and sanctioned. All the testing is done with volunteers who can leave anytime."

"Are they willing? Do you really think that?"

"What makes you think otherwise?"

As she hopped off the picnic table and grabbed her trash, she used the walk to the bin, lined with black plastic, to think of a reply.

Lying was what her mother would advise. Layers and layers of lies sometimes augmented by bribes and, in some cases, death if someone saw something they shouldn't.

But that was so old school. So passé. Adi prided herself on being a girl of the times, and in these new times, shifters and other entities were living outside the closet. Living the dream of being in the open. While her mother and aunts might not like it, Adi was pretty sure the secret of the dragons' existence would soon spill. They couldn't keep containing the sightings and videos.

Once the truth came out—and stayed out— then where would the lies get her?

Not in Dexter's pants.

She dropped the trash before turning to face him. "How do I know I can trust you, stud muffin?"

He grimaced. "My grandma ate a bran one every morning. Said it kept her regular."

Her turn to make a face. "You are really sucking the joy out of my nicknames."

"Then why not use the one I already own? Let's try starting again. This time from the beginning. Hi, I'm Dexter. But my friends call me Dex."

"And as you saw in the report, my name is Adrienne Silvergrace, also known as 'that girl.'"

"Which girl?"

She rolled her eyes. "The girl in the tabloids, you know, the rebellious, rich daughter. Blah, blah, blah. My family and I are always making headlines. Surely you've heard something."

"Nope."

"Are you sure? My family is big in a lot of circles."

He shrugged. "I don't hang in circles. IT guy, remember? We're the fellows who hang out with binary code and on forums where keeping your identity secret is a measure of your cool-kid factor."

"Ah, yes, a techy guy. Is that how you got my file? Did you steal it from your work?" Naughty boy. She totally approved.

"I didn't steal it. As part of my job, I have access to everything on the servers. Especially security issues."

"Thousands of files, and yet you happened to stumble on mine." She batted her lashes. "Ah, Dex baby. That is so sweet. You went looking for me."

"I wasn't looking."

"Why not? Don't you think I'm pretty?" She'd moved close while they talked, so close she grabbed hold of him and almost reached him on tiptoe. But it took him dipping his head for their lips to meet.

Instant electricity arced between them, a live voltage of desire that zipped through all her nerve endings.

Oh, my. The rush proved even better than that first sweet bite of a Twinkie in the morning.

More. She had to have more. Her arms wound around his neck, holding him tightly, tasting him. Fixing his scent in her mind.

We should claim this one.

Keep him for her hoard.

He would fit in nicely. Even if he was human.

Gasp. She pulled away from him and quickly shuttered her eyes, lest he see the green fire in them. A sure sign of her otherworldliness. It could be hidden by contacts, but Adi didn't like fingers poking at her eyes. So no contacts. She usually just remained calm and collected. Except around Dex it seemed. He brought out the naughty dragon in her.

But dragons and humans shouldn't mix. Not permanently at any rate like her inner beast suggested. She should move away from the forbidden temptation. Except he didn't allow it.

He cupped her face and brought her lips back for a second sweet kiss that made her wonder if the keeping of him would be so bad. Didn't her aunt have a book on the care and feeding of humans? *Make sure he gets plenty of light and that his soil is moist.* Or was that for plants? It might explain her problem keeping pets.

Who cared? She was receiving the most amazing kiss of her life. And she'd experimented quite a bit, so she was kind of miffed when he pulled away before she was done.

"Get back here," she growled, reaching for him.

Except he remained out of reach, his eyes smoky with desire, his expression hard, almost angry. "Is this part of your plan? Seduce the tech guy?"

"Can't a girl seduce a man because she's horny?"

"Not when that girl is probably using the man for something. And I don't mean sex. You want something from me. Something from Lytropia."

"Maybe I do. Nothing wrong with multitasking. Come on, pookie—"

"Ugh, that's what my grandmother calls my

mom." He stepped back from her. "Thanks for making this easier."

"So you're going to pretend you don't lust after me because you're picky about a pet name?"

"No, I'm going to have no problem controlling my lust because I'll get fired if it's found out I'm associating with someone on the company watch list."

"If you're worried about getting caught, then why take me to dinner?"

"To satisfy my own curiosity."

"I know what you're really curious about." She leaned up on tiptoe and whispered, "Tastes like cotton candy. Want a lick?"

His lips never moved, but she could have sworn she heard a vehement, "Yes!"

Pffft. The dart hit her in the upper arm, and she yelped more out of surprise than pain. She stared at the brightly-colored tuft. "Son of a bitch. Someone shot me."

The nerve. Someone would die. Or cry for their mommy. Either worked. She yanked the dart from her arm, not truly worried about it or the second one that hit her. This wasn't her first rodeo with drugs. Except her eyelids got heavy and her muscles turned to molasses. Slow-moving and sluggish. She sank to her knees, blinking, a slow open and shut of her eyes, wherein one second Dex stood there gaping at her. The next...

The next she woke to him carrying her up to her room and placing her on the bed.

And did she imagine the soft kiss on her forehead before she passed out?

Chapter Eight

Why did I kiss her? He couldn't have said. Just like Dex couldn't explain his gentleness in tucking her into her bed and drawing the covers over her.

Who is she? She was more than a bubbly-headed, rebellious, rich girl. He was certain of it, especially after tonight. Yet, no matter how long he searched online, he couldn't find a thing beyond the society pages. And everything he found only reinforced his impression.

Silvergrace daughter caught urinating in hotel fountain. Claims she thought she was in Europe.

Switching schools again? The youngest Silvergrace member has been banned from campus after allegations she posted an unseemly video to the college website. A video showing the dean behaving inappropriately with students, but still…

Adi seemed the epitome of a wild child with a mother unafraid to use the family's deep financial pockets to buy her daughter's way out of trouble.

A misfit.

A rebel just as she'd said. With all kinds of proof to back the claim.

It seemed too perfect. Something about it niggled at him. Especially after he'd found the bug. The one in his room. The one he palmed and bounced in his hand. It looked an awful lot like the ones he liked to use.

Like the one in her room right now. It was how he kept an eye on her, sleeping soundly. Almost a victim tonight, but why? Who would want to hurt her? Or was it because of who she was? The Silvergraces had deep pockets. Ransom could prove lucrative if done right.

But that theory didn't fit. Nothing about her fit. Which was why he spent longer than he should have watching her on his video feed.

It made for a restless night and a grumpy morning, especially since she'd disappeared sometime before he woke. One minute on camera, the next…gone.

Did she walk out on her own, or had something nefarious happened to her?

He couldn't explain the relief he felt when he made it to the driveway and saw her sitting in his car, two coffees in hand.

"I cringe to ask what those cost you." Having dealt with their landlady previously, he knew with ass-clenching remembrance that she charged dearly for the black sludge.

Adrienne handed one over. "Worth every penny," she muttered, her expression hidden behind huge sunglasses.

"I'm surprised to see you awake."

"I'm surprised I fell asleep," she grumbled. "I'm not usually such a snore fest. Must have been some good shit."

"About last night…I should explain. I wasn't the one who drugged you."

"Of course you weren't. Someone shot me.

The question is, did you take advantage of me?"

"No." Not because he didn't want to. But real men only did the naughty with conscious women.

"Lucky me, a man with morals." Said dryly before she took a sip of her coffee.

"Lucky for you I was there when you got drugged."

"Did you take care of me?" She shot him a grin. "What a nice boyfriend."

"I'm not your boyfriend."

"And yet, there you are, carrying me home, tucking me in after passing out. I hate it when that happens."

"You mean this has happened before? Who the hell drugged you?"

She made a sound. "Who hasn't tried? I mean, hello, have you seen the stuff on the market these days? Most of it is meant to either make a girl horny or ensure a girl is available for someone who is horny."

"That's wrong." His hands tightened on the wheel.

"Wrong doesn't mean it doesn't happen. Don't tell me you've never tried anything illegal for fun."

"I don't do drugs, and until last night, they never played a part in my dates." Too late, he realized what he'd said.

"That was a date?"

"No. I mean, yes. I mean…kind of."

"You are so cute when you're flustered."

"I am not flustered."

"If you say so. Maybe I should call you

Fluffy?"

"Aunt's one-eyed cat."

He could almost feel the heat of her glare. He held back a smile.

"I will find something to call you," she threatened. "But in the meantime, perhaps you should tell me what happened. Other than the obvious that someone was after me and didn't succeed. You saved me. I knew you hid a superhero under those ugly white button-down shirts. You kicked some kidnapper ass, didn't you?"

"Not exactly. It wasn't an attack or a kidnapping attempt. Turns out there were some biologists tracking a herd of deer in the area. They shot a tranq at a doe near the clearing for the food truck, missed, and you got hit instead." Not the entire truth, but she didn't know that.

"They hit me with some pretty potent shit."

"And for that, they apologized profusely." One of the shooters blubbering on his knees. "Once they knew you'd been drugged, they couldn't apologize enough." Especially once they'd emerged from the woods, and he had a *talk* with them. "After I settled things with those guys"—and sent them packing—"I brought you back to your room to sleep it off."

"You're saying me getting darted was just a mistake?" A glance to the side showed her wearing a frown and chewing her lower lip. "Hashtag so-let-down."

"How about hashtag count-yourself-lucky. I mean, why would you assume someone wanted to drug you?"

"Hello, awesome rich girl. And I'm cute.

Back in the day, it happened quite often, which is why I usually have a better tolerance for it."

"You say the most disturbing things."

"And you don't run away screaming when I say those things, so really, who's the fucked-up one here?"

Good question.

As he pulled to a stop in front of the nail salon, he half turned in his seat. "Are you sure you want to go in today?"

"What else would I do? I have no television in my room, and besides, weren't you the one who said it was nothing?"

Leaving her here, though, didn't sit right with him. But what else could he do? Toss her in his trunk for the day? He didn't have the right kind of rope, and the weather forecast wasn't quite right for kidnapping and confinement.

"I was more worried about inflicting you on the world." Not exactly a lie. Adi certainly had a knack for drama.

"The world is lucky to have me. Just like you're lucky to know me."

"I don't know if I'd call it luck."

"In my family, one of my aunts would say it's fate. Then Aunt Yolanda would say fate is as fate does. And then my mother would tell them any fate in our family is up to her."

"I'm beginning to think your upbringing had a lot to do with it."

"Do with what? Never mind. You can tell me later. Grab me at five."

An imperious demand that he had to deny. "No can do."

She blinked. "Did you just use the *no* word? Did we not discuss the fact that I don't recognize it?"

"I have a work thing tonight."

"A work thing that is more important than me?"

"Yes."

For a moment, he could have sworn her eyes sparked with green flame. "I see. Well, then, I guess I'll just have to entertain myself."

There was a scary prospect.

Leaving Adi, Dexter made his way to work, parking in his designated spot along with the other stiffs working for LI. The parking lot was full. No shortage of people to work in what was considered to be the most cutting edge stuff in medicine.

The day moved slow, snail slow, especially since the only exciting thing he did all day was replace some batteries in a keyboard. IT specialists didn't do all that much when the server was running smoothly, and most of it was menial—*My mouse won't work. The computer ate my report. Why won't this print?*

That was okay, though, because it gave him more time to poke around, at least when the bosses weren't paying attention. He always kept an eye open for them since they enjoyed popping in and out of offices, peeking over shoulders, making sure everyone was doing their job. Dex did his job extremely well. He was the model IT guy. He'd gotten caught sleeping once, and once more playing wastepaper basketball and surfing porn. The epitome of the lazy, uninterested employee. And they'd totally bought it.

Suckers.

Five o'clock came, and he waited a few minutes past before clocking out. He wasn't the only one. The mainstream staff also clocked out around dinnertime. Guards, secretaries, pencil pushers, those not directly involved with the science kept regular hours. Whereas the doctors and scientists tended to work late and erratic hours. Everyone wanted to be the one to make the big discovery.

I want to discover something. I want to know if LI is on the up and up or not.

Which was why he was meeting with the person who had discovered something interesting about Lytropia and wanted help in exploring it before exposing it.

Dr. Chandra Kashmir, a biogenetic engineer, had been the one to send out an SOS on the dark net looking for some help.

Intrigued, Dex answered the call.

He'd met Dr. Kashmir not long after he first arrived at Lytropia. They'd had a coffee in the cafeteria. But under close scrutiny, it had proven hard to speak, hence their meeting tonight outside town at a fine dining restaurant—which meant a menu that wasn't completely breaded or deep-fried.

"Mr. Cline. Thank you for coming." The petite woman, with her exotically tanned skin, had her long dark hair held back from her face.

"Were you followed?" he asked as he took a seat across from the doctor.

"I don't know. Then again, we both know it's almost impossible to hide with today's technology."

Given the bug he had in his pocket, one pulled out of his car, he knew all too well. "You used your colleague's car?"

"Yes. I did exactly as you told me. I had mine towed to the body shop and then borrowed Mason's old Volvo at the last moment." A vehicle without a built-in GPS. He'd also told her to pull the battery out of her phone and use a circuitous route. She was supposed to watch for any tails.

"This should help with anybody trying to listen in." He slapped his phone on the table. The app he'd activated projected a dull field that would scramble any attempts to eavesdrop electronically. "Now we can talk."

Her shoulders visibly eased in relief. "I hate not knowing when and where they're watching."

"Assume it's all the time." It was what he'd do if he were in charge of security.

"Not reassuring." Her nose scrunched. "But then again, nothing about Lytropia is. Did you find out anything from the video I sent you?"

Ah, yes, the video that had started it all and brought him here to Little Town, USA. "I've played around with it quite a bit. I ran it through as many filters as I could, but the lighting, as you well know, is bad. Whatever is in that footage is alive, but…" But he couldn't say what it was, other than not human.

"I've been poking around for another, but the folder I found it in is gone."

Probably because it was placed on the main server by mistake. "Don't go digging too hard. You don't want them to know you're on to them."

Her short nails tapped the table. "I can't sit

idly. If Lytropia is experimenting on people, then they need to be exposed."

"And what if it's not people?" he asked.

"What do you mean?" Her brow furrowed. "Are you implying that just because we're working with shapeshifters that they're not deserving of the same protection as human citizens?"

"No. But we're also assuming whatever is in that video is a person. What if it's not? What if it's some kind of animal?"

"Then why are they hiding it? You and I both know there's something wrong with the institute. They're concealing a whole other facility. Probably under the main building."

A public medical front to hide the buried illegal one. Or was it sanctioned? It wouldn't be the first time the government tried to hide less than popular actions from the public.

"I'm digging as fast as I can. Whoever runs their hidden establishment has things locked down tight. If I poke the wrong thing, he or she will know." Good programmers always had warning systems to let them know when people tried to infiltrate. That just meant he'd have to be better.

Dex needed to locate a chink in the firewall to get past the public server he controlled, to the one no one was meant to see.

He and the doctor finished dinner, discussing some of the employees they felt might have more information. He arrived back at his room late, the drive back via a circuitous route taking time. Especially since he'd stopped to grab a few things.

The last thing he'd expected when he

unlocked his door and walked into his room was to find Adi sitting cross-legged on his bed, arms crossed and looking pissed.

"And just where have you been?" she snapped.

Chapter Nine

"I was out, not that it's any of your business," Dex replied, looking all too cute in his button-down plaid shirt and thick glasses.

What he did was totally her business because Dex was her mark. He'd slipped her grasp when he left work. Her bug in his car had failed, meaning she couldn't follow.

He'd spent hours out of her sight.

The true crime, though? He'd been with another woman.

I can smell her on him. A sultry exotic scent that brought out a rage in her that she couldn't explain.

"Were you on a date?"

"No. But since I imagine you'll harass me until I tell you, I did meet a friend."

A friend? A friend who wore perfume?

Adi prided herself on being a modern girl. Modern girls totally had guy friends and vice versa. However, it seemed she also had a bit more of an old-fashioned streak than expected because, at the same time, she couldn't help but think, *Boys and girls can't be friends because they might end up getting horizontal and naked.*

He better not have. She'd kill them both.

No merccccy, her dragon lisped.

Funny how she didn't even hesitate at the thought. Even knew what it meant.

I'm jealous. How fascinating because, for once, it wasn't for a treasure in someone else's hoard. It was for someone living. A person. She wanted one person, this man, as hers.

And I don't share.

Lucky for him, she didn't smell sex. That would have totally made her snap, and she'd probably have eaten him—and not in a way he would have enjoyed.

Her arms crossed, and she almost cringed as she realized just how much of her mother she was channeling in that moment. "Exactly what did you and your friend talk about?" Forget being cool about his meeting. She simmered.

"This and that."

The vague answer did not go over well. She couldn't help but laser him with a glare. A restless anxiety imbued her, and she leaned forward. Bracing herself on her hands and knees, still on his bed, she studied him.

Perhaps more closely than she should have. She didn't feel in control. The wild part of her, the dragon, found itself so very fascinated by the man.

"Are you a shapeshifter?"

The query came at her suddenly, and she stiffened. Then her nostrils flared. "Most certainly not." She was so much more, not that she would tell him that. Some secrets should be revealed slowly. Although turning into a dragon quickly could result in some truly epic screams. She used one as the ringtone for her phone, set to a classical piece with lots of stringed instruments.

"Don't tell me you're insulted. It's a valid question. There is something different about you. Something primal."

"Are you accusing me of having a beast inside this body? Not my fault you bring out the sex kitten in me." She purred the words as her head cocked, a chunk of pastel hair layering itself over half her face.

"That's not what I mean, and you know it. I don't know what you are." His steady gaze proved unwavering, fearless. "I only know what I see. You don't move like other women."

He'd noticed? Her chest puffed out.

"You don't say what you should."

Because she wasn't afraid to speak.

"And your eyes…"

"What about my eyes?"

He shrugged. "It's like they have green fire inside. But only sometimes."

He'd seen her inner fire. That shouldn't have been possible. Usually, she kept it hidden from the humans. It was the first thing she'd learned as a dragonling. Never let anyone see.

Except, around Dex, she seemed to have lost her control. He appealed strongly to all the parts of her. Including her dragon.

Want him. It was enough to trigger heat in her, and she crawled to the very tip of the bed. Close enough that she could reach out and touch.

"And there it is, like green flames glowing." He murmured the words, and she realized she'd done it again, not even realizing.

She shuttered her orbs, striving for some

semblance of control. The man flustered her. Kind of embarrassing really, considering he wasn't even a cryptid—the word dragons used to describe those who weren't quite human.

At least a cryptid mixing with dragon had interesting results—look at Aunt Faye with her half-mermaid, half-avian daughter. She'd become a flying fish who could only go outside in the rain. A very odd existence.

For dragons, coupling with a human produced wyverns. They could look human, bore no scent, and had the ability to flip into a more lizard version of themselves. Scaled, and winged, they resembled teen dragons caught in the phase before they ascended. Forever trapped and never becoming.

Male wyverns were further cursed, as they couldn't procreate with others. Not dragons or humans. Not any known cryptid actually. Closer examination showed their genetic strand almost identical to a dragon one. They'd had scientists map it in an effort to cure the male dragon shortage—no one knew why they bore more women than men.

The doctors had found something they thought was the reason why wyverns were wyverns and not dragons. A teeny-tiny chunk of genetic material was missing. An important piece, apparently. A piece that, when missing, made a mating impossible.

She realized Dex waited for her to reply. To tell him why her eyes burned.

"I am not a shapeshifter." The absolute truth. However, if one were to argue, dragons did indeed shift shapes. They possessed three forms they could morph into—a human form that would pass most basic tests. They could also pull what was known as a hybrid shape, which was humanoid in appearance with wings and scales. And if they truly wanted to prevail, then they called upon their majestic dragon. Large, and yet light because their bones, while immensely tough, were hollow. Unlike land-based creatures, where water had proven an important building block, dragon molecules contained more air. It made them buoyant, allowing their big shapes to fly. Now if only they could find a place they could soar without getting shot down or worrying about hitting a plane.

Ah, for the days their kind ruled the lands. A long time ago. Those cities and empires had long since fallen. Mostly at the hands of humans, but dragons had played a part, too. The dragons had begun decimating each other within their own ranks long before humanity rose up against them and tore down their mighty cities.

We were queens and kings. They were the power. So why then did the dragons hide? And why did they keep denying they had anything in common with the cryptids who had been outed to the world?

We hide because we are, at the core, afraid of getting wiped out again.

The news was full of stories of people going on the hunt for fairy tale creatures. All Parker's fault, and now that bastard had disappeared.

The whole world looked for him. Humans because they had questions about the supposed monsters living among them, and the shifters because they wanted him to stand trial for his crime of revealing the truth.

The dragons wanted Parker because he didn't fear them and had threatened to tell their secret to the world. *If we find him, then I expect we'll tear his head off and drink his blood before setting his remains on fire until he is nothing but ash.*

That was the most surefire way to ensure Parker never returned in any shape or form. The world might not know it yet, but the dead didn't always stay dead. It wreaked havoc on the digestion at times.

"There is something different about you."

"Yes, there is. About time you noticed." She gripped the edge of the mattress and leaned forward until her face was mere inches from Dex's chest. The shirt would prove no barrier if she decided to have a go at his skin.

He gripped her by the shoulders and lifted her until they faced one another.

"You're avoiding the question. What are you?"

"What am I?" She repeated the words with a smirk that grew. "I am the center of the world. Everything revolves around me. It's a weird fact that scientists don't understand."

"If they know of it, then how come this is the first I've heard of it?" He teased her right back, his hold on her having slid to her waist.

The pressure of his palms on her lower back excited. Especially since both his thumbs stroked. Up and down.

A simple movement. Very simple. Over clothes at that. But people didn't stroke things they didn't like.

He likes.

I like, too. She ran a finger over his jaw, the fine goatee and mustache a soft burr. "This is going to tickle when you go south."

"Ladies aren't supposed to be so forward."

"I'm not a lady."

"Says a girl born with a silver spoon in her mouth."

"Pumpkin, you have no idea how true that is."

"I hate pumpkin. All squashes actually."

She might have hissed.

"And the devil must be guiding me because I don't hate you." The nicest thing he'd said. The grudging tone really brought a tear.

He didn't want to like her. The man fought it really hard, so the admission—oh, yes, the admission that he did—warmed her heart. Grabbed it in a big, giant, squeezing hug that she felt in her girl parts.

A mini orgasm, that was what that tremor was. Did he know? The hands on her body pressed more firmly, his fingers digging. He drew her closer and higher, bringing their lips close. So fucking close.

"I don't hate you either." She whispered the words, knowing the heat of them brushed his mouth.

"This is wrong." Said as his bottom lip dragged across hers, a feather-light touch. It brought a tremble to her entire frame.

"Wrong is good." Wrong made it hot. She grabbed his lower lip with her mouth, giving it a little suck before letting it go.

He rumbled, a yummy, growly sound. "I don't have time to be distracted."

"This isn't distracting. I'm doing exactly what I should be." Her arms draped around his neck, and she let her next words whisper across his mouth. "I'm going to do you."

Her hands skimmed down his body to his shirt. A collared shirt tucked into black slacks. He wore the casual geek so well.

He pulled off his glasses and tossed them to his dresser. "That's better."

"Don't you need them?"

"Not full-time. Just for certain types of work."

"Is this your way of saying this isn't work? I don't know if I'd agree because you're making me work for it." She bit at his lower lip, pulling it.

A rumble came from him, low and sexy. "You're making this hard."

She grabbed hold of him, the *hardness* of him. "Yes, it is. I know what will fix that." It would fix the same problem she had when he was around. She slanted her lips over his, rubbing them and drawing a response.

"Fuck me." He probably meant it as an expletive.

But she took it quite literally. She took his mouth, took it with a passion greater than that for her Twinkies.

Screw cake. She was tasting a man. A man with commanding lips that gave as good as they got. Nothing soft about his embrace. And his tongue…

The way it could twist and turn, she couldn't wait for it to hit the dance floor below her waist.

She grabbed hold of his shirt, two fistfuls, and tumbled back on the bed with him, dragging him atop her.

He didn't stop the tumble, landing heavily on her, but his hands took some of the brunt, meaning he didn't completely crush her. Pity. A good smoosh was fun.

With his heavy weight atop, her body shuddered. There was something delicious about having a man over her. A taboo submission to another.

Her legs parted, and he dropped down, nestling between her thighs, a welcome, heavy weight against her lower parts.

They were both still fully dressed, and yet that didn't seem to matter. He kept rocking his hips against her, the rigid length of his shaft pressing against the seam of her pants, putting delicious pressure on her clit and sex.

His mouth meshed with hers, their breaths panting and hot. She moaned as he rocked against her again, felt her pleasure coming, that buildup, that pressure.

The bed creaked as she urged him on, faster and faster, the rubbing so exquisitely lovely. So exciting.

Small, gasping moans escaped from her, and a low rumble rolled continuously from him.

It was coming.

I'm so close to coming.

So close.

So…

Bang. Bang. Bang. "Stop the fornication this instant!"

What?

Chapter Ten

The vehement knocking on the door and the shrill yelling saw him drawing away from Adi with a frustrated growl. Close, so close to spilling his seed like a young man who'd yet to learn any kind of control.

The word control didn't seem to exist around Adi. She had this ability to weave an erotic spell around him, and he couldn't resist it. Actually, he found himself more and more vulnerable to her crazy charm.

Bang.

"Ignore her," Adi whispered, trying to draw him back for a kiss. "She's just jealous because she's got cobwebs in her coochie from disuse."

Probably. "We should stop."

"We'll stop when I say we stop." Said with such vehemence while her eyes glowed with green fire. Unnatural fire.

She isn't human. And he wasn't sure how he felt about that. Until not long ago, he would have chalked her up as being different. Interesting.

Now, he knew there were things not quite human in the world. *What is she?* The fact that he didn't know served as a reminder that this woman had a secret, a possibly huge secret. He needed to not cave to the raging desire consuming him because he wasn't sure how he felt about getting involved with someone not quite human.

Not true. His dick was more than happy to dip into whatever she had that passed for a pussy.

His mouth was more than happy to kiss her sweet lips.

But his mind, the mind that couldn't help but wonder if sex with her might kill him, was glad the landlady had interrupted their make-out session before the clothes came off.

On the other hand, Adi didn't seem happy about the intervention. "Go away. We're busy. As in about to get naked and sweaty busy, so bugger off," Adi shouted.

Wrong reply.

"Unclean whore. Lord, oh Lord, save me from sinners. Especially the whore plying her sinful ways in my home. Get out of my house, Jezebel, and leave that nice gentleman alone."

"I am not a Jezebel." Adi rolled off the bed and stood. "They wear much sluttier clothes," she confided in an aside to Dexter.

Did she have any idea how appealing she looked with her short hair mussed, her lips red and swollen from their kissing while her skin still held a pink blush?

Bang. "Open the door this instant. You are out of here, hussy. I do not condone this type of behavior under my roof."

Before he could stop her, Adi swung open the door. "Why hello there, Mrs. Givry. Have to say, your timing really blows. You interrupted things just as they were about to get climatic."

He could have choked at her words. They were just a touch brazen.

Mrs. Givry drew herself up—all of her five feet—and adopted a stern mien that would make many have nightmares. The face of a righteous warrior on a mission. "I told you when you rented the room. No fornicating in my house. Especially not with strangers."

"Dex isn't a stranger. As a matter of fact, we're getting to know each other quite well. And, secondly, we were not fornicating. We were making out, and it was pretty damn awesome. As in, I was going to come at least once, probably twice. Until someone rudely interrupted." Adi narrowed her gaze on the landlady.

Laughter wanted to burst free from Dex at her audacious speech. She truly had no shame and really believed the world revolved around her. She certainly did shine as bright as the sun.

"I want you out of my house." Mrs. Givry pointed in the direction of the stairs.

"Leave? I'm afraid I can't do that. I have work to do here. You'll just have to learn to turn up the television. Or you could take some pills to sleep. I have a feeling we could go all night." She tossed him a wink, and he had to hide a guffaw behind a fist, turning it into a forced cough.

"Out!" The screech reached epic proportions.

A normal person might have left at this point before things truly got out of control.

What did Adi do? She turned and took enough steps to lean in for a peck, a quick smack of her lips against his and a husky, "This has been fun, but I've got to run. I have some business to take care of tonight, pudding."

"Name of my cat who got run over."

"Dammit." She scowled at him. "I will find something. You'll see."

The landlady made a loud noise. "Enough. Get out."

Adi whirled from him and tossed her head in a gesture more reminiscent of a queen than a punk pixie. "I am not leaving, old lady. I paid for a week, and I am getting a week. Or would you like me to call my lawyers and have them sue your ass for breach of service and harassment?" Adi left with a slam of the door, but he could hear her arguing with the old lady. Finally promising to, "Tell you what, I will not fornicate with the saintly Mr. Cline in your house, but outside of it, I will do my best to put my dirty, dirty hands all over him."

What a twisted promise to make. Not that it mattered. He'd stay out of her path while he did his job here. He couldn't afford her as a distraction.

Mrs. Givry interrupting was the best thing that could have happened because he'd almost given in to temptation. Who was he kidding? He had given in, and would have gone all the way if not stopped.

Even now, long after Mrs. Givry's steps clomped down the stairs, he listened. Listened for a sound.

Heard nothing. Adi didn't come back to finish what they'd started. And that pang he felt? Surely not disappointment.

Time wasted, and he had a job to do. A job that might prove time-sensitive. Dr. Kashmir might have stumbled on the biggest clue thus far that Lytropia was hiding something, but if someone knew she'd found out, then…things like files might suddenly disappear. He had already copied the files he had access to for evidence before someone wiped everything. But it was the files he'd yet to find that he truly wanted to get his electronic digits on.

He stripped down to his boxers and a T-shirt before he sat crossed-legged on the bed. He flipped open the lid on his laptop and booted it up.

While it went through its various checks—spyware, firewall, abnormal poking of any kind—he thumbed through the stack of comic books by his side. The code to log in would require careful calibration. A calibration he'd devised that needed a word in one of the comics. Only one word decided by date and time. The log-in screen appeared. He checked the clock and plucked an issue out. Next, date. He flipped to the page, counted seconds for the words, finger quickly skimming and arrived at "fuck-a-licious."

The screen unlocked, and he had access to the most sophisticated piece of machinery on earth. One wrong attempt to log in? The thing self-destructed.

Coolest thing ever. And, yes, a total boner moment for the geek in him.

He took a peek at the general stuff first. Emails—two were for jobs, one to let him know of a completely unsanctioned sale of government cast-offs, including the next generation of bionic tech. A mix of metal and man. A true miracle of science.

I'll have to put a bid on that. He wouldn't mind

integrating an upgrade or two to his body.

Next, he took a gander at the server over at Lytropia. Dex took care of the day stuff. Ricky took care of the night. The institute made sure there was twenty-four-hour IT help. The scientists worked all hours of the day with no concept of time, and took great exception when help wasn't readily available.

A rather dull fellow who spent most of his shift playing WoW, Ricky never even noticed that Dex logged in and took a stroll around the binary world of the LI server.

As per the previous times, nothing to see. Nothing to indicate any behavior out of the ordinary for a place like this.

On the surface.

But in the world of code, so much could hide just below that. With careful peeling and circumventing, Dex was wiggling his way through the top layer of security to the hidden world below.

There is a bigger network out there. I can see it. Could see the edges of it but had yet to find a decent-sized chink.

It meant careful probing. Think of it as a fence around a property, a barrier lined with cameras, motion detectors, and even checks for sound. Get past that, then there was a pit, lined in stakes, followed by a moat with monsters. The perils went on and on, but each time he tackled those barriers, he delved a little further, a littler faster. He created a zigzagging fissure that would take him to the heart of the secrets.

Tonight is the night I make it all the way inside.

He cracked his knuckles and went to work. Hacking was an addictive pastime. Success took skill and patience. To infiltrate someone else's digital castle was a very precise thing. It meant pitting yourself against the protective proficiencies of another.

The goal became penetrating the opponent's layers of defense and then, once inside, declaring victory. And then pillaging everything.

Total fun.

Fingers tapping, Dex went deeper than he'd ever gone before. His eyes behind his glasses glazed—the lenses helped him to focus, a neat tech he'd bought for a pretty penny on the black market. They somehow helped focus his gaze on the important things as he waded through the code. They gave him an advantage in the ultimate puzzle game.

It's almost over. He could feel it. Almost see the end in sight. He hovered before the final hack, he was sure of it. He'd found the door to the hidden digital world of LI.

And he wasn't alone in front of it.

The code on the screen moved, even though his fingers were still. He stared at it for a moment before slapping furiously at the keys, countering the code. Someone was working against him. Someone attempted to steal his hack.

You are not taking this away from me.

Oh, yeah? the countermeasure seemed to say. *Watch me.*

He didn't watch. He reacted. Dex had not gone this deep to give everything over to someone. If anyone went through the binary door to the other side, it would be him.

He and his adversary proved evenly

matched. Their coded swords swinging, causing their goal to seesaw in front of them.

It was truly a brilliant battle. However, the flurry of activity online set off an alarm. "Ah, fuck, no." The curse did nothing to help him. The remote server shut down, knocking him offline.

Not good. Not good at all because that meant whoever ran the dark side of things knew someone had come looking.

More than one someone. *I wasn't alone in there.* Which made him realize something startling. *Why do I get the impression I know who that was?*

A flip to the camera for her room showed a benign scene, her just sitting on her bed, reading. Barely moving. He flipped back, but something about it bothered him, so he flipped over again to see her still reading. He didn't believe it. He was sure it was her hacking against him. He couldn't have said why, other than that his gut insisted. The very idea she'd ruined his digital penetration was almost enough to make him march across the hall and demand answers.

Almost. Then he remembered her eyes. Those inhuman eyes.

Beautiful, truly gorgeous, especially with her pixyish features. But not fucking human.

Which meant she was lying to him, and he didn't like that one bit.

So he stayed in his room and did nothing but listen to his aching blue balls that accused him of being a dumbass.

Chapter Eleven

Poor Dex looked like he needed an IV of coffee the next morning.

"Rough night?" Adi asked. She'd slept pretty well once she'd pulled out her handy-dandy pocket rocket. Travel-sized and always a source of entertainment at the airport checkpoints. She vividly remembered the exchange.

"No, sir, it's not a bomb. Would you like me to demonstrate its use right here, right now?"

Good times. She took a sip of her coffee as he eased the car out onto the street.

He didn't peek at her. At all. "I had a work thing that didn't go well."

Was he going to whine about it? "It would have been fine if you'd backed off. I had things in hand."

"So it was you." He slammed on the brakes, jolting her. She also spat some coffee on his dash. Oops. He wouldn't like that.

"Just so you know, I don't usually spit."

"Don't change the subject. I knew it was you. You're the reason we got locked out of the server."

"Me? If you'd not bumbled around in there and let me do what I had to, this never would have happened." Grabbing a tissue from the box he kept in the console, she dabbed at the wet spot. The tissue stuck, white and coffee-stained sludge glued to his dash. Maybe he wouldn't notice.

"How the hell did you come to the conclusion this is my fault?" He stared at her for the moment, probably stunned by the realization he was wrong.

"Because it is. It can't be mine. I'm the center of the universe. I don't do anything wrong."

He gaped at her, obviously in awe. Humans were easily impressed. "You never told me you were a hacker."

"I prefer the term professional information extractor. Also known as PIE. I offer an all-you-can-eat buffet of services. *Crème de la crème.*" She winked. Just in case her innuendo proved too subtle.

"What happened to you working at the nail salon?"

"I do. Lovely place, shitty tips. Apparently, I only get to keep tips if I do appointments. What kind of gimmick is that?"

"But you're not just a salon worker. You were on the LI server last night. Why?"

"Why not? In my spare time, I like to fly my drone and scare the shit out of my family, eat really artery-hardening stuff, and hack secure networks and hoard the secrets I like. Never know when some of it will come in handy."

"You hack for personal gain?

"Mostly fun, and maybe a bit of world domination." She shrugged. "But that one is more of a long-term game." All dragons aspired to become, once again, what they'd used to be.

"You should have stayed out of LI."

"Why? You certainly didn't."

"I work for Lytropia. I am half of their IT department. It's my job to spot leaks and plug them."

"I've got something you can plug." She parted her thighs and shot him a suggestive glance, which was totally wasted since he stared straight ahead.

"Last night, I might have given you the wrong impression."

"You mean that wasn't a massive erection pressing against me while we were making out?"

"No. I mean, yes, I was aroused, obviously, but only because you threw yourself at me."

"Only because you apparently don't know how to pounce a woman and ravish her. I don't mind showing you."

"I think you've shown me enough."

Dex, baby, I haven't even started.

Her battery work of last night had worn off, and her girl parts throbbed as if she were an untouched virgin on her first date.

I want him so badly. Instead, she fished a Twinkie from her pocket and opened the package so she could take a big bite.

As she chewed on a sugary replacement for the man beside her, she wondered if he noted her eyes were muted today, the color a dull and boring hazel. She'd had to resort to her lenses today because her mother harangued her at length last night about a report of a girl with green fire eyes riding a bull. The pictures were all over the Internet.

And Adi was easily recognizable. Everyone assumed the images were tampered with, but her mother knew better and warned her appropriately.

"Wear your lenses or that black piece of plastic you carry around will be useless."

She wore the lenses rather than lose her credit card access. How else would she buy her snack cakes?

"You need to stay away from the LI server."

How cute. She took another bite as Dex continued his warning, which, she might add, she had no intention of heeding.

"If I catch you doing it again—"

"What makes you think you'd catch me?" She licked the icing from her lower lip, and she noted his gaze strayed from the road a moment longer than it should have, becoming fixated on her moist mouth.

"I'd catch you."

Perhaps he would. He'd proven himself canny. He'd found the bug in his room and his car. Found them and yet hadn't said a word. Just like she'd found his and made sure she gave him only a little show. She wanted to tease, and draw him close, not give it all away for nothing.

"Tell you what, Dex baby. I'll stay away from your precious computers if you have dinner with me tonight. Somewhere with a dark booth." She grinned as she ran a finger up his thigh. "If you're modest, then choose a place with a hanging tablecloth. Personally, I don't mind when people watch."

At the way his jaw tightened, she knew she'd

touched a nerve. A couple of them, she'd wager. She brushed a quick kiss on his lips before hopping out of his car. She couldn't resist a parting, "Have a good day at work, honey bunny," before slamming the door shut.

He leaned across the car, and the window rolled down. "That's what we called the class guinea pig."

Her smile turned to a scowl. "Hashtag so-not-funny."

"Later, gator."

Gator? Someone would have to explain himself. Was he implying she had scaly skin? *Touch it. You'll see I'm soft and silky.*

And when a dragon, her scales were even more perfect. Not at all rough and bumpy. While tough, her scales were smooth to the touch, like silver armor all over.

Stalking the sidewalk to the salon, she wandered into a yelled, "You're late, new girl."

Was that human talking to her? Adi fixed her gaze on the owner, stared hard enough to make the woman fidget. "I don't think so. Think about your attitude while I go to get some breakfast."

"Take your time."

Duh. She already planned to. Only once she filled her belly did she return and deign to take some appointments, more out of boredom than anything.

The nail salon proved to be a bust. At this point, her time would be better spent elsewhere looking for clues.

Say like with Dex.

He could use a partner. In bed. Out of it. She

kind of wanted both. But a certain deadline loomed.

I wonder how he feels about sex with a pregnant woman?

Because they would have sex. Copious amounts of it. Soon. Tonight if she could wrangle it. #sexgoals.

"Yo, princess, look lively. You've got a client."

With a sigh, she leaned up in her seat and took the towel off her eyes. Way to ruin an almost nap.

A woman wearing a god-awful, blinged-out windbreaker thumped into the seat across from Adi, and Adi's nose twitched. *I know that smell.*

"Aunt Waida, is that you?" Because the brassy-haired woman in front of her with the yellow smile, nicotine perfume, and overly rouged lips looked nothing like her usually hippie-styled aunt.

A large wink met her. "Name is Tonya, darling, but my friends call me Toni."

Oooh, Auntie was playing undercover. What fun. "Hi, Toni, what brings you to town? I don't think I've seen you before."

"Just here visiting my sister. She recommended I check this place out. How's your hand with tweezers, girl? I could use a good plucking."

"You need help with that unibrow problem? No worries. Right this way." Adi ushered her aunt into the cubicle meant for privacy during plucks and waxes.

She turned on the ocean sound machine, used to relax their clients before the pain started. Adi then hissed, "What is going on? Why are you here pretending to be some old lady?"

"I am an old lady."

Adi waved at her. "But not this old. Why are you here? Did my mother send you? Jeez, I told Aimi to tell her I had this under control."

"She didn't send me. Didn't anyone tell you I was already in town?"

"Yes, but I didn't figure I'd see you. And it's not like I called and asked for help." She didn't need help. Adi just needed some time away from the house before it became her prison.

"No you didn't call, and yet you should have the moment you woke from that drugged dart. I should tan your behind for that."

"How did you know about the darting incident?"

"Because I was watching, of course. A Silvergrace princess comes to a town suspected of cryptid experimentation…that means someone needs to watch lest your foolish carcass get taken."

"I wish. Things around here have been kind of dull." Workwise, but when it came to her love life, things were looking up.

"Dull? What about the night they drugged and tried to take you?"

"You mean that big snafu with the wildlife taggers? Boring."

"You have no idea, do you?" Aunt Waida shook her head. "Silly child."

"Are you giving me one of those weird prophecies again? I thought you stopped working for that psychic hotline."

"I stopped that back in oh four. Once it went online, it just didn't have the same panache."

As Adi talked to her aunt, she grabbed some tweezers and went to town. Her aunt tended toward a more hippie outlook on dress style, but in some cases, such as that of these bushy brows, natural was not better.

"You never did explain what I have no idea about." If Adi had missed something, then she needed to know.

"That Dexter boy, he's not who he says he is."

Duh. He had many ooey gooey layers, and she was enjoying peeling them back. *Then I'll get to lick his insides.*

"What do you know about him? Because I've yet to find anything out." All the Internet trolling and database hacking wasn't getting her the answers she needed. The public profiles all claimed he was a gifted hacker who lived with his mom. Seriously. His address—on his website listing his services for hire—stated basement for an apartment number.

"Your boy is more involved in the situation than he's letting on. You should team up with him."

When Adi thought of teaming up with Dexter, she thought of doing it naked, and it involved some sweat equity, a lack of oxygen, and combustion.

When her aunt said it, she meant as in seriously, as in work. "Team with a human?" Her nose wrinkled. "And here I thought you were going to say I should eliminate him for knowing too much."

"What does he know?"

"Nothing. Yet. But he suspects me of

something." Probably super awesomeness.

"You need to get closer to him."

"How close?" Because to get any closer, she'd have to wear him like a skintight Dexter suit.

Her aunt's eyes blinked, and for just a moment, the slits of them stared back, green with dragonfire. "You need to get close enough to ferret out his secrets."

"Gotcha. Squeeze him until he coughs them up. And what will you be doing in the meantime?"

Big yellow teeth gleamed as her aunt grinned. "I'll be digging over in yonder hills. I hear there's buried treasure."

Trust a dragon to ferret it out. #gimme.

Chapter Twelve

As soon as Dex walked into Lytropia, he noticed the unusual activity in the lobby. People walked about in small groups, heads huddled, whispering and casting suspicious glances at one another.

He sauntered to the front desk to the check-in manned by Bobby—a soldier wannabe with his crew cut hair, stern bearing, and perfectly pressed guard uniform. Interestingly enough, he wore a sidearm, not a baton. Open carry state and the institute hired only those who had a permit.

Is it packed with silver bullets? One day he intended to find out. For the moment, though, he played his role.

"What's going on? Did the new girl get caught in the copy room with Horatio?" Dex asked. He had five bucks riding on them doing it by Friday. The whole office had money riding on the pair doing googly-eyes.

"Haven't you heard? Our system was hacked last night."

All that attention for an attempted hack? They happened all the time—to other people. Dex ran a tight server.

LI didn't, so poor Ricky wasn't able to hide

the attack, especially once the server shut down and didn't come back up. All the computers went into a stripped-down safe mode. No one could access a thing, and Ricky didn't know how to fix it. Judging by his panicked texts, which Dex had ignored, Ricky was worried he would be fired since he couldn't get anything back online.

Yes, Ricky, you will probably be fired. Someone's head will have to roll, and yours is just the right shape. But Dex didn't say this to Bobby. Instead, he executed a perfectly compassionate reply. "Shit, man. I can't believe it. Someone hacked us? Good thing Ricky was on staff to fix things."

"Ricky can't fix shit," said the guard. "Fucking moron is blubbering and snotting as he works. He doesn't know what he's doing, and the bosses are pissed."

I'll bet they're pissed. What use was an IT guy who couldn't fix things? He shook his head. "That blows for Ricky. Good thing I'm here. Time to teach those pesky machines a little respect."

"You should get the cameras back online first. It's hard to do my job blind."

"I'll see if I can unravel this mess," Dex said with a smile before heading off.

He found it interesting that whoever ran the shadow server had shut things down so tightly, in effect drawing more attention, instead of slapping on some tougher firewalls. The fact that he'd revealed himself meant he'd have a harder time getting in. And his window had just become smaller. If the hidden part of LI felt threatened, who knew what they'd do?

The computer lab—also known as his

office—held more people than it should, which made him cringe as they weaved among the computer towers. Who were these guys in serious button-down shirts and latex gloves, unhooking the computers and boxing them? Others, men in plainer clothing comprised of charcoal colored T-shirts and khakis, carted them away.

What the fuck is going on?

This wasn't the usual procedure for a computer hack. Usually, in the case of a break-in, all outside access, and even interior network access was shut down. Then the IT department tracked the hacker's trail and tried to figure out what had been seen or taken. They also built a barricade to prevent a future hack through the same hole in the defense. That was how things worked.

You don't get rid of the computers.

He watched for a moment before pushing his glasses high on his nose and stalking in with an indignant, "What are you doing?"

A man wearing a navy blue suit turned. Having met him when he was hired, Dex recognized the Lytropia CEO. Gunther Morales. A man who'd come out as an admitted wolf shifter, married to a human with three kids. Not puppies, the media announced—with a hint of disappointment. According to the pediatrician—not a veterinarian—only one child showed the shifter gene.

"We are removing these machines and putting in new ones. A precaution given that the server was compromised last night."

"A breach doesn't require new hardware." Dex called bullshit when he saw it. "Surely you know we can prevent it from happening again with a software plug."

"No need. It's my fault for not investing in a more recent set of computers. Last night's infiltration attempt has only reinforced the belief that we need to switch over to a newer, more secure system."

"But you'll need time to replace these. What will happen for the time being?"

"Luckily, we began preparing a while ago." The wide smile seemed friendly, but Dex noted it didn't reach Mr. Morales's flint-gray eyes. "The company won't be down long, as the new units will be arriving tomorrow."

More bullshit. Dex wasn't a moron. He knew how things worked, but he wouldn't learn anything rocking the boat. "What can I do to help?"

"We need to shut down and disconnect all the computers. We have staff working on the machines on the first floor. Why don't you start doing the same for the units on the third floor."

Nothing more than an errand boy. How deflating. But on the upside, Dr. Kashmir was on the third floor. Maybe she'd have some clue as to why the drastic step.

Leaving his office, Dex noticed fewer people buzzing around. The computers might be leaving the building, but most of the scientists had laptops or tablets. They'd simply jot their findings for the day in there.

The elevator spilled him onto the third floor, and while he wanted to skip the first few offices and labs, who knew who watched his actions? He had to give the appearance of not doing anything suspicious or out of the ordinary. LI was on a witch-hunt. So he started with the room closest to the elevator. It didn't go well.

After a few arguments with the scientists—one even cried when Dex pulled out the plug—he made it to Kashmir's lab. She wore a white coat and was bent over a machine, staring at something.

All around, things hummed, and stainless steel surfaces gleamed. Cleanliness was paramount in testing conditions.

"Ahem." He cleared his throat when she didn't immediately notice his presence.

Her head lifted, and upon seeing him, she was less than subtle in her stare.

"Sorry to disturb you, Dr. Kashmir. I've been given orders to shut down all the computers on this level."

"Shut down? What for?"

He rolled his shoulders as he sauntered over to her computer. "Someone tried to hack us last night, so upper management has decided we need to swap out these machines for new ones to prevent it from happening again."

"That's insane. How am I supposed to work?" she exclaimed, but as she spoke, she scribbled on a sheet of paper. *We need to meet. I found something.*

"I guess you'll get to leave early today. That actually sounds good to me. They've got two-for-one appetizers at that Western bar downtown. Only from four to six, though."

"Do they serve wings?" She jotted, *I saw something big with wings last night.*

His eyes widened. He didn't for one

moment doubt her. "Best wings in town. You should check it out." He clicked off her screen before he stood. "Your computer is off-limits now. The guys will be up here shortly to grab it."

The dull outward conversation covered the exciting sub one. She'd already scrunched the paper she'd written on and tucked it in a pocket. Given the camera was at their back the entire time, no one should have seen a thing. Which made him wonder, was security active during this computer swap? Perhaps not in this building at any of the guard desks, but he would wager the flip side of this institute kept a close watch on things.

Once he'd left the doctor, it didn't take long to shut down the remaining machines, and then, with nothing to do, because they wouldn't let him box or carry any of the electronics to the truck, he got to leave early. Which meant he was an hour early for the wings, so he had to go easy on the beer.

Four o'clock came with a half-price basket of wings and rings. The first beer was followed by a second. Five o'clock hit, and he found himself eyeing the door. Still no sign of Kashmir. He tapped his foot. Adi expected him. But he wouldn't be there.

It occurred that, while they might have exchanged some fluids, he had no way to contact her. He'd never thought to ask her for a phone number, and he most definitely hadn't given her his. That didn't stop his phone from ringing at quarter after five—belting out an old eighties title, Salt-N-Pepa's *Push It*. He answered, knowing who it had to be. "What did you do to my phone?"

"Is that any way to greet me when you're late to pick me up? A more appropriate reply would be, 'sorry, Adi. I am the lowest form of creature right now for being late.' Followed by your arrival in a burning screech of rubber."

Her mind-boggling retort almost had him laughing. "How did you get this number?" And how did she change the ringtone? He had his smart device retina scanned and fingerprint protected.

"Did you seriously ask a hacker how? I have my ways."

Nail artist his ass. How had he fallen for that? The woman had some mad skills if she could get his encrypted number. No one had it. If LI wanted to contact him, they went through a rerouted shell number. "I don't know you at all, do I?"

"Nope. I'm a mystery, a mystery who is standing on the side of the road, waiting for her ride. My patience is wearing very thin."

"I was unavoidably detained."

"By what?"

"I promised a friend I'd meet them."

"You ditched me for a friend?" The incredulity almost made him wince.

"It was important."

"I'm more important." She sounded quite indignant.

"This is starting to stray into weird territory." He noticed a familiar face enter the bar. "Listen. Sorry about the ride thing. I've got to go. My friend just arrived. I'll talk to you later." He hung up before she could launch into another rant. A shame because her rants often went in fascinating directions.

As Dr. Kashmir took the seat across from him, her features flushed. He activated his anti-spy app on his phone.

"Sorry I'm late. For some reason, Mr. Morales wanted me to stay and talk to him."

"What for?"

"I don't know. He never showed for the meeting, and I got tired of waiting and left."

"Were those guys done boxing the computers when you left?"

"Yes. They left not long before I did, but as I drove away, I noticed a new cube van arriving."

"Was anyone still in the building?" Because he'd noticed the lot was pretty empty when he left.

"Everyone was encouraged to take the afternoon off. Mr. Morales said we would be closed for the evening to allow the cleaning crews access to our labs for in-depth sterilization. Apparently, not having the computers there makes it safe from a security standpoint."

"Sounds hinky to me."

Her shoulders lifted and fell. "On the surface, everything they say makes sense, but I can't help thinking something serious is happening. Perhaps they are looking to shut down."

"Seems that way." He'd find out more when he got home. "You looked agitated this morning when I saw you. And you mentioned seeing a thing with wings."

"I did, as I was leaving the lab last night. I heard a strange sound and looked up. Overhead was a big shape. *Really* big. With wings."

"There are eagles in this area. They can get

pretty large."

She shook her head. "No. What I saw was bigger. Much bigger. But that wasn't my biggest news. I think I found the way into the secret lab. Turns out it's not right under LI like I thought. Although, there is a tunnel."

That piqued his interest even more than strange flying monsters. "Where is it?" He leaned forward.

"It's—"

"That's your friend?" For a tiny woman, Adi had a voice that carried, and she also possessed great tonality. Everyone in the place could hear the displeasure in her words.

He stood from the table as Adi stalked over, every inch of her lithe frame agitated. "What are you doing here?"

"Not meeting a woman in secret," she snapped back.

"It's not a secret. I told you I was meeting someone."

"That's not a friend. That"—she jabbed a finger at Dr. Kashmir—"is a woman. A very pretty woman. In a bar. With you." She veered her gaze back to him, and he was surprised to see no fire in her eyes today. As a matter of fact, her eyes seemed dull and less vivid than usual.

"Dr. Kashmir works with me. She had a computer issue that she needed help with."

"And do you always repair computers over beers and wings?"

Standing, Dr. Kashmir tucked her phone into her purse. "Listen. I don't mean to cause trouble. And I just got a text I can't ignore. I can talk to Mr. Cline about this tomorrow at work. I really have to get going."

The doctor made to leave, but Dex held out his hand. "Don't rush off. We should finish our talk."

"I really can't stay. I'll contact you later." To Adi, Dr. Kashmir offered, "Nice meeting you."

Adi crossed her arms, her expression that of a woman scorned. "I'd say the same, but that would be a lie. Keep your claws off my man."

"Your man?" he hissed when they were alone. "I'm not. We're not anything."

"Yet. But you will be honored to know I've chosen you."

"For what?"

"Anything I desire."

"Well, la-di-fucking-da for you. I, on the other hand, have no interest." An utter lie. Even now, pissed as he was at her for stalking him, he wanted to kiss her and grab her and punch the guy ogling her ass from where he sat at the bar. Get him close enough, and he had an app to wipe the fellow's accounts clean.

"You have no interest in me?" Her eyes widened, and she laughed. "Don't be silly. Of course you do."

"You interrupted a perfectly innocent meeting with your jealous fit."

"You deserved it. You shouldn't have ditched me to meet another woman in secret. If I didn't know you liked me more, I'd have hurt you by now."

He scowled. "I don't like you."

She didn't respect the scowl and leaned up

to nibble his chin. "I know you think you don't right now, but that won't stop you from fucking me hard before the end of this night."

"The only thing I am doing is going back to my room to sleep."

"Yes, you'll probably be tired when you're done."

"I am not doing you."

"Arguing isn't very attractive. So smarten up. I won't have it said that you're not pretty. And I won't tolerate grumpy."

"I am not grumpy."

"You are, but that's okay this time." She patted his cheek. "It's because you're horny. I know how to fix that."

That's what I'm afraid of. And that fear propelled him from his seat and sent him running to the door.

He didn't escape.

Chapter Thirteen

Dex thought he could run. Adi had news for him. She'd had an epiphany when she'd seen him having a *tête-à-tête* with that woman.

Adi feared nothing. Not flying. Or fighting. Not even her mother on a rampage. Yet, seeing Dex in close conversation with another woman? It had twisted something inside her. Made her blood run cold.

What if I lose him? The very idea truly put things in perspective. What if some other whore tried to take Dex from Adi?

Killll her. Simple, cold logic.

She should start with the pretty doctor. Contrary to what Dex said, she knew that woman— Dr. Kashmir, if she remembered her research correctly—was totally making eyes at her man.

My man. Mine. Her dragon seemed quite certain about that.

Adi, though…there were many reasons not to get involved with him. So many, starting with the fact that her mother would never let a daughter of hers take a human as a mate. Ever. Then there was the whole twenty-eight thing.

Since when did she care about the rules? Adi hadn't become rebellious by towing the line.

Exactly why was she fighting her desire for him? From the moment she'd spotted Dex, she coveted him. She wanted him, not only for a few nights of pleasure, but longer. Maybe even forever.

Screw the fact that she was close to twenty-eight and her mandatory breeding time for the family. Her mother expected Adi to present herself in a few weeks' time for the first round of fertility injections. *But I don't want to go.* She didn't want to have to explain to Dex why her family expected her to get artificially inseminated. She didn't want to have to justify to anyone the size of her Twinkie hoard if the embryo took root.

Why can't I just live my life? A life with Dex and no forced pregnancy.

Wanting him for more than just a night was the most rebellious thing she'd ever even contemplated.

But she wasn't doing it just to spite her mother.

I want him.

Now if only Dex would stop playing hard to get. Using the *no* word with such futility. Didn't he know that only made him hotter? His resistance was such a sham.

Because he totally wants me. He just wouldn't admit it, so it was time to force the issue.

I'm gonna squeeze the truth out of him. Or squeeze him just for fun. Bet she'd make him squeak—in a good way, of course.

Exiting the bar, Adi noted him striding down the street to his parked car. A car she'd spotted as the vehicle she'd commandeered—a pizza delivery guy who didn't mind making twenty bucks—passed it on his route to take her back to the boarding house.

She saw Dex's hunk of junk and screamed, "Stop." She didn't mean to make the poor fellow pee himself.

Since she actually had some tip money on her, stuffed in a pocket, she threw some bills at the driver for the ride and pizza—deliciously laden with toppings and cheese—before spilling out onto the road. It didn't prove hard to find Dex after that. Her dragon showed her the way. The rest was history, which was why she stalked him—with clicking heels and sassy attitude—to his car.

He didn't turn around once; however, she could tell by his too-relaxed posture he was all too aware of her presence. Time for him to stop ignoring her.

"Oh, Dex baby, I'm not done with you." She practically sang the words.

Having reached the bumper of his car, he whirled. "Yet I'm finished with you."

"We aren't done until I say we're done. Remember who the world revolves around, sunshine."

"Sunshine, used by my kindergarten teacher and the lady at the grocery store with the mole on her chin."

She saw what he did. Tried to divert her attention and break the erotic tension tugging at them. "It is futile to resist."

"I can't get involved with you."

"Why not?" Her head cocked to the side.

"Because I don't have time for the type of chaos being involved with you would entail."

"Do you really think it would involve anarchy?" She couldn't help but clap her hands in glee. "Do you have any idea how much fun that sounds?"

"What did I do to deserve this?"

"You were born." She grinned, a wide grin. It might have held a bit of hungry nymph in it. It matched her naughty words. "You're also pretty. I like to keep pretty things. And *pet* them."

He couldn't completely hide the shiver that went through him. "I am not a thing. You can't just decide you'll take me."

"Why not?" She reached him and pushed her body against his until his ass hit the trunk of his car, bracing their weight. Her hands bracketed his hips, palms flat on the cool, hard surface. "You're available. Visually appealing and…" She leaned in close and sniffed him, inhaled his aroma, and her head tilted back. Her eyes closed. She reveled in his scent. "Delicious." The word emerged almost on a purr.

The edge of her jaw brushed across the fabric of his shirt, feather-light, not even enough pressure for him to feel it on his skin, and yet he stiffened, his whole body turning into unyielding stone.

You will give in.

She blew hot air as she moved up his body. To give herself leverage, she braced her palms on Dex's chest, but he grabbed them and pulled them to the sides.

"No. I don't even know what you are."

Did he not recognize it? She finally did. "I am your destiny."

To his credit, he didn't laugh, as it did sound kind of corny. But neither did he have an epiphany and declare undying devotion—or at least pledge his ardent admiration with his tongue on her clit.

"How can you say that when we've only just met? We're practically strangers and opposites to boot."

"Yin and yang, a perfect pair. But, at the same time, we also have many things in common."

"Like what?"

"We both have an admiration of me."

"It's not admiration; it's disbelief because you're delusional. We are not a thing."

"There's that *no* word again. Stop denying it. I know you see it, too."

"I see nothing. Because there is nothing. I don't want you."

"Liar, liar, pants on fire. Let me take them off you." She pulled her hands free and grabbed at the waistband of his trousers.

"Stop that."

"Make me." She rose on tiptoe and nibbled his chin.

With his hands braced on her shoulders, he held her back. "This is totally unladylike."

"And you protest too much." She chopped his arms and broke his hold, but she didn't pounce him.

"I'll keep protesting because you're still lying to me. There is something different about you, and I won't get involved until you tell me what it is."

"Demands. Demands. Perhaps I am special. Perhaps not. It doesn't matter. This thing between us is real and not going away."

"I wish it would," he grumbled, but without any real heat. He let out a sigh. "You're fascinating but also very scary. I'm not used to my women being so—"

"You will not use the term 'my women' again. Ever." Or she might kill him.

"Are you the crazy jealous kind? Is that stunt you pulled in the restaurant going to repeat itself?"

"Most definitely." She shrugged. "I can't help it. I tend to be a tad bit protective of my hoard."

"Hoard? As in treasure? You don't own me."

"But I will." Confidence was one of her many gifts. Tenacity, too. She moved close to him again, close as she whispered, "I will make you feel things you never imagined. If you let me."

"Damn you." He grabbed her, pulling her tautly against him. With a sound that was part groan, part growl, he crushed his mouth to hers, plundering her lips with savage hunger.

About time.

A storm unleashed in him, a tempest comprised of passion and frustration. He poured it all into his kiss as his hands palmed and claimed her ass.

"Get a room!" someone shouted.

Why bother with a room when there was a perfectly fine car with a solid trunk? She wound herself around him, her skirt riding up on her thighs as she pressed herself against him. Her hands reached between their bodies.

"We shouldn't do this in public," he murmured against her mouth.

"Prude." Outdoor sex in public was epic.

"And we can't go back to the boarding house," he said in between licks and nips of her mouth.

"I will kill you if you stop," she growled.

"Come with me." He pushed away from the car and carried her a few paces into an alley. Not a dirty alley, but, still, not a bed.

"Here?" she questioned. "Why, Dex, you dirty, dirty boy."

"Shut up," he growled.

"Make me—" She lost her breath as her back hit the wall and he pressed himself against her. And she meant pressed.

His mouth claimed hers with scorching intensity, a meld of their flesh that heated her blood to boiling. His hands roved, tickling her skin as he touched the band of exposed flesh between her top and skirt. His hands pushed under the fabric of her shirt, his thumbs stroking across the underside of her bra. Her nipples poked, hard nubs begging for attention. Pleading for his mouth to suck.

His thigh pressed between hers, shoving the fabric of her jeans skirt up, up until he could rub his leg against her core. She wore panties today, a small scrap of fabric quickly soaked.

She couldn't help but groan against his mouth as he rubbed his thigh against her, teasing her and making her breath catch.

Her fingers dug into his scalp, tugged at his hair, and he uttered a grunt of satisfaction. Someone liked it a little rough.

Her lips pressed firmly against his, as if she could brand him by sheer force and will alone. A part of her, and not just the dragon part, wanted to claim this man, to imprint herself on him so intensely he forgot about ever pushing her away again.

A raging inferno consumed them, every wet slip of his tongue against hers, every rub of his hands on her flesh, the crushing press of their bodies, all fuel for the fire. Heat flushed her head to toe. The layers of clothing impeding the connection of their flesh irritated, especially since they refused to burn to ash.

He stood in the middle of the alley, so he had plenty of room to maneuver. His hands spanned her waist and lifted her, and he murmured a soft, "Wrap your legs around me."

Yes. She straddled him, spreading her legs enough to draw his body between her thighs and then locking her ankles around his waist while her arms remained looped around his neck. His big hands shifted to her ass, her jeans skirt pushed around her waist. She still wore her flimsy thong. He curled a finger around part of it and tugged.

Rip.

"Dex!" She said his name more out of shocked excitement than true despair.

"I'll buy you a new pair." His lips rubbed against her, soft and sensual, as he added, "And I'll probably tear those, too."

Wetness. Holy wetness. She might have come a little at his words. She definitely trembled as he ground his pelvis against hers. He still wore pants, though. That seemed the height of unfairness.

She reached a hand between them; she

found the first button and freed it. No zipper. Buttons all the way.

Pop.

Pop.

Pop. And out it sprang, his briefs unable to contain his erection. She grabbed, he moaned, and his hips arched.

"Mine." She might have said it out loud, and she didn't care as she guided it to the opening of her sex. The rigid head of his cock pushed against her, and the idiot muttered, "We need protection."

"No, we don't." She couldn't wait. Everything was hot and ready right now. She wanted to feel him sinking into her. Driving home that lovely long cock.

His hands adjusted their grip on her ass as she wrapped her legs tighter around him, drawing him into her snug, damp sheath. He stretched her so nicely, the width of him a delightful pressure against her channel.

She stopped breathing for a moment at the sweetness of his penetration. The pure delight.

Tightly, she gripped him with her arms and legs. Slowly, he seated himself the entire way, and holding back looked as if it was torture to him. She watched him as his head leaned back, the cords in his neck bulging with the strain. The temptation proved too much, and she latched her lips to his skin, sucking at the spot where his pulse beat. Biting, not hard enough to break skin but surely sufficient to leave a bruise.

He didn't mind, not judging by his groan.

"You feel so fucking good." A guttural moan of words that caused her to clench. He shuddered.

She wiggled her hips, and his whole body trembled again.

"I can't hold back." His growled warning before he began to truly pump at her. His hips thrust back and forth as his hands on her ass cheeks controlled her, bouncing her to and fro against him.

Sweet. He pumped her hard and fast, slamming his fat cock in and out of her. She couldn't help her mewling cries of pleasure. Her bliss snapped and coiled within her, absolute torture and perfect pleasure at the same time.

The moistness of her flesh eased his way, and yet, at the same time, her sex gripped him tightly. Squeezed him like a fist.

He inhaled sharply. Gasped and changed his angle. Slowed his pace. He tilted until he found her G-spot. Then he began to tap it.

Her fingers clawed at his back as he bumped her sweet spot, over and over. Pleasure made her blind. Bliss stole her breath. Ecstasy made her convulse in silence.

As her moist flesh pulsed around him, he stiffened, his body arching forward and deep into her, so deep. He let out a yell of his own before spilling his seed hotly inside.

He held her. Held her close with a body that trembled and shivered and panted just as strongly as hers. Dex cradled Adi close to him, so close. So perfect. His face buried in the soft curve of her neck.

It wasn't her fault it seemed like the perfect time to say, "Bite me. Hard enough to draw blood. Let the world see I'm yours."

Apparently, that wasn't the right thing to say.

At all.

If ever a man repented sex, it was Dex. She might have been more insulted if it wasn't such good sex.

He'd be back for more, and it would be hot again because he'd fight it.

They drove back to the boarding house in silence, his expression contemplative. Someone wasn't in the mood to talk, and she allowed it. She felt rather mellow herself.

Could use a smoke. Her dragon didn't mean the cigarette variety, though, but rather a true burning fire. She especially enjoyed the smell of hickory.

He pulled into the drive and turned off the engine. It ticked for a moment as the hot motor met the cooler evening air.

Since Dex sat there, not moving, she sat with him.

At length, he finally spoke. "What happened hasn't changed anything."

On the contrary, it changed everything. Did he not feel that tendril now connecting them? A gossamer link that she didn't think could exist between a dragon and a human. *How come they didn't tell us we could mate a human?*

Was that what she'd done? Had she truly taken him? Could it be seen?

He certainly didn't seem any different now that he belonged to her.

Since words would change nothing, she simply leaned over and planted a kiss on his lips.

Felt his startled breath, his lips opening and ready for more…

She heard his groan of frustration as she bounced out of the car and left him hanging. It made her grin. #stillwantsme.

She skipped into the house, offering a quick wave to Mrs. Givry, who watched with narrowed eyes from her chair in the living room.

"Good night, you old bat. I'm going to bed. Alone." *I kept my promise, silly human. I didn't fornicate under your roof.* But she probably would in her dreams.

#soakingthesheets.

Chapter Fourteen

What is she doing?

The question of the hour because he didn't know. The bug Dex had planted in Adi's room showed only one thing. A piece of paper with a message, for him.

Sleeping naked, thinking of you.

Lucky. At least she slept. He'd spent the night lying awake and horny, reliving the sex in the alley over and over.

More than just sex, it was an epic, possibly life-changing moment because he couldn't deny it anymore.

He really, really, really, fucking really liked Adi.

Fuck.

And he liked her even though she wasn't one hundred percent human.

She felt human enough last night.

But that didn't mean shit. What if she turned into a monster? Would he be able to look past a monster to the woman underneath?

He wasn't sure of that reply, which, in turn, bothered him. How could he be with someone that might revolt him later?

What if she was a monster?

What if…

The one thing he did know was that he craved her. Now. Again. Possibly even worse than before. Once just wasn't enough, and he doubted twice would be either.

I need to talk to her. See her. Something. And yet, the sign over her video feed didn't move, and her door remained shut when he exited his room. He almost knocked. Stood before her door with his fist raised, but that smacked of desperation. Besides, she was probably already downstairs sitting in his car with some of that awful coffee she liked to overpay for. He almost leaped down the stairs in his haste to go see, only to find his step slowing to a stop as he noted the seats in his car were bare.

It took him by surprise enough that he sat behind the wheel, engine running, waiting to see if she'd appear. When she didn't, he couldn't delay any longer, not with his phone blowing up with messages from folks at LI.

Something big was happening at Lytropia Institute, and if he didn't want to look suspicious, he needed to check it out.

The first difference he noted upon pulling into the gated facility was that the parking lot was only half-full, the usual rank and file of vehicles pitted with empty spots. He grabbed his work briefcase with his laptop, covered in geeky stickers such as *I <3 to byte*. His true device he kept tucked under a carpet in his car in a specially made, recessed chamber. Every day, he found a furtive place when he left his room for the night to make the swap.

Upon entering the building, he could hear

the angry buzz. Employees were pissed and not afraid to show it. They had a right to be annoyed. Something odd had happened that went beyond the computers getting pulled yesterday.

There was equipment missing. Lots of it. Big, expensive machines that had worked fine the day before. Add to that there were no updates. No one could locate a memo, and it seemed there was no upper management to harass for answers. None of the suits had come into work.

The science types who showed up were pissed, so, of course, they took it out on him.

"When is my computer getting replaced?"

"You're putting me behind on my research."

"Where is my oscillator?"

"Are we getting fired?"

That more than anything was the fear on everyone's mind. Were they still employed? Would they have a check to collect at the end of the week?

Dex didn't have the answers. Nor did he care to look for them, not when it became obvious no one would provide any. So he stirred the pot, just for fun, as employees milled around. He started a rumor in the cafeteria about a supposed leak. A leak that Dex claimed came from Saunders' home computer. Apparently, an online porn site he was hooking up with managed to put a Trojan on his machine and sold the information to the press. People, especially the women, were outraged.

In another rumor, he made it out to be corporate espionage with Ricky as the ringleader.

He had tons of fun sending folks on a wild goose chase, enough that they soon left him alone to his own devices. Not that he could do much. His laptop wasn't a substitute for a proper server, but it did have a mirror of many of the files, which he absently poked at while chewing on some Chinese food he'd found in the fridge.

He poked through emails, looking for any discourse from the management level about what had happened. He looked for some kind of warning or explanation. He found nothing, and yet he wasted hours looking. Most people fled the building before lunch, and he couldn't have said why he hung around, other than to see if anything would occur.

Could a large business like Lytropia really just fold overnight without a word to anyone?

A warning bell went off on his computer. He put aside the kung pao chicken and took a peek.

Dark Pegasus connected.

Who the hell was Dark Pegasus? And how had they tapped into his machine? While not his super secure laptop, he had a few bells and whistles to keep the casual poker out. He tapped a few keys and began perusing his system log and immediately cursed. Someone was wiping all of his Lytropia information. He had backups, but still, this was unexpected.

And unstoppable.

Whoever had hacked the hacker had launched an epic clean program. He could only watch as folder after folder disappeared from his drive.

His wasn't the only laptop affected. Those who remained in the building and attempted to work as if nothing had happened started filing into his geek space again with laptops sporting the blue screen of death, and in some cases, when he took a deeper peek, all he could find was a drive, neatly formatted, wiped entirely clean.

A hidden Trojan suddenly activated?

How very high-tech and James Bond-esque. He wanted to applaud the skill of it, especially since he'd never spotted it.

And neither had Adi. His phone rang, and today it sang *Like a Virgin* by Madonna. He almost blushed.

He answered. "What?"

"The proper response would be, 'good morning, hot stuff. I missed you this morning.'"

How did she know? Being a man, he didn't admit it. "Took the day off, did you?"

"More like many days off," she grumbled. "Can you believe they fired me? Just for that, I might buy that salon and fire them."

Solutions of a rich girl. "I'm kind of busy right now." He wondered if his cloud-stored versions of the Lytropia servers were safe. Would the virus activate in them, too? He'd kept the LI stuff separate from his personal data, but…he'd have to be very careful.

"Something wiped my computer."

Her admission had him replying, "Me, too. Everyone in the company is reporting problems with their personal machines and, for some, their phones. Anything electronic connected to the company is being wiped."

"Your phone still works."

"But the bogus phone account I was given by human resources? Yeah, it's been disconnected, and all my texts on it erased."

"And so it begins again," she said as if musing aloud. "It's just like what happened to Bittech."

He straightened in his seat at the name. "What do you know of Bittech?"

"Just that something similar happened to them after Parker dropped out of sight. One day they were open for business, and the next morning, employees arrived to work and found nothing."

No power. No notice. No warning. Just instant job loss. He already knew the facts. What he found more interesting was that Adi did, too.

"I think it's time we talked. Really talked." Time they both laid their cards on the table because he got the feeling more and more that they might be striving for the same goal.

"Sounds like a plan, sugar muffin."

"Don't use the S word around my mom. She's diabetic."

Adi might have made a rude noise. "I will find something, meatball."

"Hate them on my pasta." He grinned as she yelled.

"Come pick me up downtown at the 7-Eleven. I had to hitch a ride for food. Mrs. Givry isn't selling overpriced snacks anymore."

"I'll be there in twenty."

More like ten. He drove faster than the speed limits posted for once and soon pulled to a stop in front of the store with every snack known to man. Adi stood with a bulging bag in each hand. She opened the back door and put the bags on the seat, and he noticed the peeking edge of a familiar treat.

"Did you get anything other than cake?" he asked as she got in.

"And ruin my palate?" She seemed aghast. He, however, couldn't live on cream-filled cake alone. Dex stopped in at the grocery store and grabbed himself a meringue pie—for his fruit quotient of the day—a few boxes of hot rods—for protein—and a milkshake to keep his bones strong. With most of the food groups covered, he returned to his car to find Adi flipping once again through his comic books. Comics he'd hidden in his secret compartment under the carpet well. She'd found it.

His gaze narrowed, but he didn't say anything until they'd pulled away from the grocery store.

"Why are you really here?"

"Because you have a car, you're cute, and I need a ride. On you, not the car, just in case that wasn't clear."

He ignored the erection as he went for a better answer. "You're doing it again. Trying to throw me off."

"Why would I do that when we'll get better results with you on top? Or, even better, inside?"

"Why are you here, in this town? What's your interest in Lytropia? Who are you, really?"

"What do you think?"

His fingers tapped the steering wheel. "Your online footprints indicate that you're a rebellious rich girl always getting into trouble with the law. But that's just a façade. I want the truth."

"So do I."

"What's that supposed to mean?"

She snorted. "Now who's playing dumb? I

mean, like the fact that you act as if you're some geeky nerd who works a real job instead of the truth—you're a work-for-hire hacker who specializes in industrial espionage. Oh, and you have some serious fighter moves."

"What makes you say that?"

"My Aunt Waida finally sent me a video of the night I got darted. You lied."

He had. Those fellows had been trying to kidnap her, and they'd tried to take him, too. But they'd missed with their dart. He hadn't with his fists, and the careful application of a gun to a forehead had gotten him blubbering answers. Mostly along the lines of, "We were hired to capture you both and drop you here for cash." Only ten grand.

It was rather insulting, which was why he'd left the wannabe ransomers alive to live with the shame of working for so cheap. He grinned. "Took you long enough to figure that out."

"Your real name isn't even Dexter Cline."

"Dexter is my middle name. My real name—
"

"Doesn't matter. You'll take mine when we wed."

That caused him to swerve on the road. "What?"

"I know you heard me because, according to your last checkup, your ears are fine."

"Slow down. No one said anything about getting married."

"Fine. We can live in sin. Mother will hate it, but then again, she will be predisposed to hate you on principle."

"Why will she hate me?"

"That is a big conversation for another time. Right now, I'm more interested in knowing who hired you to go after the Lytropia Institute."

Lie about the fact that he'd been hired? No point, she knew what he was. "No one technically hired me. This is actually a pro bono project. Dr. Kashmir is friends with someone I know. She sent a certain video and suspicion to him. Since my friend was otherwise occupied, I offered to come check things out and see if her claims were valid."

"You have a video? Show me." Adi turned in her seat, eyes wide with excitement.

"Let's get back to the boarding house first. And you'd better be prepared to give a little, too."

"I plan to give you a lot." She made a sucking sound, and he sighed.

"We don't have time for that. Not with things escalating."

"There is always time for a quickie."

True, what would five minutes, ten if they fooled around a bit first, really do? Get them kicked out at the least since the landlady wouldn't like it.

As if reading his mind, Adi snapped, "Screw Mrs. Givry."

"She wouldn't be so uptight if someone did."

For a moment, there was silence in the car, and then she snorted. She giggled, too. "I think that is the funniest thing you've said so far, Dex baby."

"Then you haven't been paying attention."

"Oh, I've been watching," she growled. "That's probably how I missed that Trojan on my machine. My aunts are already mocking me mercilessly."

"Your family knows what you're doing?"

"My family is always sticking their snouts where they don't belong. Seriously, you'd think I was a complete newb at this shit the way they treat me."

"So you're here not just for hacking fun but because you're looking for information. Why? Who is it for?"

As he pulled into the driveway of the house, she leaned over and pecked his cheek. "You'll have to squeeze me if you want more information. Naked," she added before hopping out of the car.

He took a moment longer to exit, willing a bit of limpness to his friend below the belt. Coming around the front end of the car, he noted the landlady's Cadillac sat in its usual spot. Odd because he'd been told Thursdays were Bingo night and to ensure he didn't forget to lock the front door if he went out.

Mrs. Givry was really big on locking things. Especially the front door. Apparently, a woman on her own couldn't be too careful about home invasions. He didn't point out that she didn't have anything worth stealing.

Knowing Mrs. Givry's stance, he found it very peculiar the front door was unlocked. He wasn't alone in noticing it. Adi stepped in front of him, barred him from the door with an arm.

"Hold on, Dex baby. Something isn't right. Someone's in there."

"Maybe our landlady has company."

"Mrs. God-awful has no friends, and the only way her family is showing up is for the funeral to dance on her grave. Stay behind me."

Could there be any words more emasculating than that? Wait, there was the act itself that made his manhood shrivel.

She pushed open the door and stepped in. Silence blanketed the house. For once, the canned laughter of a sitcom didn't echo from the living room off the front entrance.

Adi stepped out of sight, and he quickly entered behind her. Immediately, the hairs on his body lifted. An odd smell permeated the air.

"What is that?"

"Sssomething that doesssn't belong here." She hissed and lisped her words. "Get outssside."

"Like fuck. I'm not leaving you in here. You think something's happened." Adi knew it, just like he'd known it the moment he spotted the unlocked door.

"I sssmell blood. Lotsss of it." The odd announcement led to Adi moving past the living room to the kitchen with its pristine counters and empty table.

There was a closed door at the back, the landlady's private quarters. As if Adi cared. She flung open the locked door with a hard turn of the knob. *Crack.* Something broke, and the portal opened into a haven for quilted fabrics. From the multi-hued bedspread to the stitched squares of the rug on the floor. There was even a quilted tapestry depicting flowers on the wall. What he didn't see was any sign of the landlady. He also couldn't smell the blood Adi claimed she could.

Something creaked overhead. Adi's head tilted, and she stared. The sound didn't come again, and yet, he tensed, ready to move.

"If you insist on staying, you might want to pull that gun out of the holster on your ankle."

How did she know? At least Dex didn't have to explain it. He pulled the weapon free and clicked the safety off. Clutching it with two hands, he pointed it at the ceiling as he followed Adi, who once again took the lead.

It became obvious that Adi, despite her usual flighty ways, knew what she was about. She moved with the stealth of a predator—the only thing missing was the glow of her eyes.

She padded up the stairs, managing to do so without a single creak. He didn't even think that was possible, which was why he took care to follow exactly in her footsteps. No use warning someone of their approach.

As they neared the top of the stairs, he finally caught his first whiff of copper. *Not copper, blood.*

This wasn't his first operation that involved violence. It made him wish he'd gone for the golf clubs in his bag—code word for rifle. Calvin wasn't just his buddy; he was also his weapons supplier.

A body lay on the floor, half in, half out of his doorway, the thin legs riddled with blue veins, the housecoat having ridden up when Mrs. Givry fell.

"She's dead," Adi announced softly.

Recently, too, he'd wager, given there wasn't any foul smell signaling decomposition and other bodily functions that happened once life left a body.

But how had she died? Adi stepped over Mrs. Givry and entered the room, whereas Dex stopped and knelt outside the pool of blood that spilled around Mrs. Givry's upper body.

The jagged tear at her throat probably hadn't taken long to kill the landlady, who appeared to have interrupted someone in the process of searching his room. By *search*, he meant they'd torn the place apart. Ripping pillows and scattering the stuffing, tearing open the mattress before flinging it over clothes and drawers dumped on the floor.

Thump.

The sound didn't come from the body or Adi or him. He turned to look behind him, at the closed door to the other bedroom on this floor.

They weren't alone.

He rose and moved to the other side of the hall, to the right of the door, his gun ready. Adi leaped over the body and, without any kind of slowing or finesse, kicked the door open. She also strode right in.

"Stop right there," she snapped.

She'd found someone! He flipped into the open doorway, gun held out, only to pause and blink at what sat perched in the window, perfectly framed by the falling twilight.

A head with a ridged spine flowing down from between pointed ears, along the length of its back to the tip of its pointed tail. Thick, black claws gripped the sill. Talons sharp enough to slice a throat, he'd wager.

Its skin appeared scaled, a tough, dark leather, but the freakiest thing, freakier even than its pointed yellowed teeth, the human orbs staring at them from its skull.

"What the fuck is that?" he said in a low

voice, not daring to move his gaze from the thing.

"I honestly don't know. But I'm going to guess we should either catch it or kill it."

At those words, it hissed, showing some kind of comprehension. It also had some speech since it uttered a guttural, "You die."

It leaped out of the window, and Adi ran to it. Bracing her hands on the sill, she grumbled, "It got away. Dammit. Mother won't be happy."

"I'd think your mother would be happy that thing didn't get its claws in you like it did Mrs. Givry."

"Oh, please. I could have taken it. I'm tougher than I look." She smiled, and in that moment, given the feral nature of that grin, he believed her.

"What are we going to do about the body?"

She blinked at him. "You mean you're not going to call the police or contact next of kin?"

He snorted. "Uh, no. I am not into dealing with the paperwork and the questioning and all that other shit. Plus, can you imagine explaining that some kind of demon imp killed her? Yeah. I'd be locked in the nearest psych ward for seventy-two hours if I did."

"Body disposal isn't usually my forte."

"The fact that you're even calling it body disposal is kind of disturbing."

With the negligence of a queen, she waved a hand. "Don't get squeamish on me now, Dex baby. Obviously, we're hot on the trail of something. Otherwise, why search our rooms? They're after something."

And there was only one thing he could think

of.

"It must be me." Adi sighed. "The last attempt was foiled by you, so they were here to lay a trap and capture me."

"By searching my room?"

"Obviously they know we're involved, so yes, that would make sense." She smiled, quite pleased with herself.

He shook his head. "More than likely, they're looking to see if we have any backups of the files we took from Lytropia. My guess is there's something they don't want us to see."

"Did these amateurs really think I'd keep it here?" She looked around the bedroom. "I mean, this isn't 2014. We don't use USB sticks anymore. Not when you can put it to a cloud and make many simultaneous backups at once." She rolled her eyes, and she'd never looked or sounded sexier.

It almost made him say, "check out my cloud," but the body in the hall made the moment kind of awkward.

"I've also got copies, off-site, of course. But I'm worried about the Trojan activating on them."

She sniffed the air, once, twice, then frowned. "You should worry more about that smell of gas."

"What gas?"

"The natural gas I smell seeping from downstairs."

"We should get out of here." He turned for the door, only to feel her grab him and yank him off balance in the direction of the window.

"No time. We have to get out right now."

He took a gander out the open window,

noted the hard ground two stories below with nothing to break his fall, and shook his head. "I'll take my chances on the stairs."

"Don't worry, Dex baby, I got this covered."

Then she tossed him out the window.

"What the fuck is wrong with you?" he yelled on the way down.

Chapter Fifteen

What the fuck is wrong with him?

He still wasn't talking to her. Not even a single thank you for having saved his life.

Sure, he'd probably worried a bit when she tossed him from the window; after all, humans weren't meant to fly. Adi could, though.

She'd jumped out after him, caught him, and made sure they hit the ground with her taking the brunt of the impact—on account of her bones being able to handle it.

If she were a guy, it would have been called chivalrous. Because she was a girl, he'd called it, "emasculating." And then he wouldn't talk to her as he stalked over to his car.

He made it only a few stomping paces before a bright orange light lit the windows on the main floor of the house.

Kaboom. The structure exploded with extreme force, wood and siding and glass fanning out in a wave of destruction.

She managed to turn her back and shield her face with her arm to escape the brunt of it; however, Dex wasn't made as sturdy as she.

Smoke billowed as flames crackled, hungrily eating the dry interior of the destroyed house. She ran to where she'd last seen Dex. She didn't see a body, or parts of a body—always a good sign.

When she did find him, he was on his knees, kneeling beside his car. His crushed car.

The force of the explosion had sent the chimney toppling, and since his car was parked closest...

She put her hand on his shoulder. "She had a good, overly long life."

"She can't be gone. Maybe a body shop can—"

A burning hunk of wood on the hood crackled and popped, sizzling the paint.

"She's dead, Dex baby. And good riddance. Wait until you see what a car made in the last decade can give you."

He ignored Adi and moved to the driver's side, wrenching on the door.

"Let it go. Walk away." He continued to yank. "I don't think it's drivable," she said, not that he listened.

He managed to pull the door open and did not speak as he scrounged around the footwell of the driver's side.

"Fuck. It's gone."

She didn't need to ask what, given she knew all of his hidey-holes and what he put in them. "They took your computer?"

"You knew it was there?"

"Duh. It's not like you made it hard to find." Especially since she had the advantage of being able to smell it hiding.

"Dammit. Apparently, I need to start locking my car." Which sucked because since when did people rob pieces of junk? He raked a hand through his hair and stared at the dancing flames crackling in the house. "This is bad. Really bad. Someone is on to me. Us. I need to call Kashmir and warn her."

Adi allowed it since she was more interested in sniffing around, ignoring Dex's strange looks in her direction as she tried to decipher just what she'd encountered in the house.

Dex wasn't far off when he'd called it an imp, except, as far as she knew, imps didn't exist. Then again, according to humans, dragons didn't either.

The world wasn't the same place she'd known a year ago. However, one thing she could state with certainty? Whatever that thing was, it wasn't natural, and she mentioned it to her sister from a hotel room she and Dex managed to rent— the sudden shutdown of LI having created some vacancies.

"I'm telling you, that thing wasn't right. If you'd seen it, you'd understand what I was saying when I called it messed up."

"Do you think it was an experiment let loose by Lytropia?" Not such a far-fetched idea, given that Aimi's very own mate, Brandon, was the result of some genetic splicing done by Bittech. But where Brandon was a gator shifter spliced with some dragon, the creature Adi saw was different. So very, very different.

Apparently, Dex had noted the problem. "It had human eyes."

"Most cryptids do, and those that don't, always use contact lenses," she observed aloud so that both her sister and Dex could hear.

"Is that what happened to your eyes? I knew I wasn't fucking nuts," he accused. "You're a crypto-thing, aren't you?" Given he glared at her, she knew it was time to hang up.

"I'll call you back. I gotta have a fight with my man then have make-up sex."

"Have fun. It will probably be the last time before Mother tries to drag you home," Aimi noted.

The reminder of the ticking clock didn't sit well.

Adi hung up and tossed the phone on the bed before she faced Dex. He was freshly showered and wore only a towel. With the moisture still beading and rolling down parts of his chest, she couldn't help herself from licking her lips.

Yummy.

"I'm not food."

Oops, she'd spoken aloud. But who could blame her? In that moment, she'd have traded her entire cake collection just for him.

"You might not be food, but I still want to eat you."

"Don't change the subject. I want to know what happened to your eyes. Why don't they shine with green fire anymore? Are you wearing contacts?"

She'd offered to give him oral, and he wanted to know about her efforts to blend in with humans? She poked at her eyes, one at a time, and pulled off the lenses. She blinked. "Better?"

"I'll be better once I know what you are."

"Do you really want to know?" Because she got the impression he didn't. Dex seemed mightily perturbed with things that didn't fit into what he considered normal.

And I am definitely not normal. Thank goodness. She doubted she could stand the boredom.

"I deserve the truth." Before she could reply, his phone rang.

"Don't answer it."

He answered it. "Yeah."

With her enhanced hearing, she could hear a panicky woman's voice on the other end. "I think I messed up. They're on to me."

"Where are you?"

"In the woods. I went looking for that thing I was telling you about."

Adi realized it had to be Dr. Kashmir calling, and she didn't sound too happy. Neither did Dex.

"Idiot! Why would you do that?" he exclaimed. "Give me your coordinates. I'll come get you."

Her man, rescue another woman? "I'm coming, too." Forget the fact that she'd not had her shower yet. No way was she letting Dex have the pretty doctor thank him with perhaps more than words.

The doctor saved them a trip. "Don't bother leaving where you are. I'm at my car. It's best if I meet you. Where are you?"

Dex told Dr. Kashmir then hung up and began to pace. "She must have found the location of the secret lab."

"I love secret labs. They are the bomb." Not that Adi would know, given they all blew up before she found them. Maybe this time would be different?

"I should get dressed." He whirled and grabbed at the clothes he'd managed to salvage from the trunk of his car.

She didn't have any clothes. At all, since she'd stripped out of them and stalked him, naked.

His eyes widened as he saw her coming. He'd lost his glasses in the commotion, and she missed them. She totally wanted to pull them off his face and toss them to the side before dragging his face down for a kiss.

"What are you doing?" he asked. "We don't have time for sex."

"Yes, we do, but that's not what I need." She stepped past him, running a finger over his bare chest. "I smell like burning asphalt shingles. I'm taking a shower. A nice *hot* shower. I'm going to probably touch myself in there, too. My hands skimming over naked flesh."

"Adi." The utterance of her name held a pained tone. "It's not nice to tease."

"I never claimed I was nice. And who says I'm teasing? We probably have at least fifteen minutes before your precious doctor arrives. Plenty of time if you know what you're doing."

She stepped into the still steamy bathroom. A quick crank of the faucet and the water pumped out of the showerhead, still piping hot. Even with the roar of the water, she heard the door to the bathroom click shut.

He'd left.

The coward. A real man would have dropped his towel and got in with her.

She braced her hands on the tile wall of the shower and leaned forward, face ducked so that the water poured over her head in a torrent. The noise of it must have muffled his approach.

She didn't scream, though, at the touch of his hands on her waist. Awareness let her know who touched her.

Dex had returned, and without asking, without arguing, without any kind of preamble, he gripped her by the hips, kicked apart her thighs, and pressed the thick head of his cock against her sex.

"You drive me fucking wild." The words were reluctantly pulled from him, but there was nothing reticent about his erection. He pushed into her, the thickness of him stretching, and she welcomed it. Her buttocks arched to allow him better access. Her body trembled that he would just take her, like this, in the shower, and from behind.

How decadent.

He slapped his cock in and out of her, a pounding of flesh against flesh that had her screaming his name quickly. Oh so very quickly.

Her climax hit, brilliant and strong, and it triggered his, the hot seed of him spilling, his fingers almost bruising as he clutched.

The moment utter sensual perfection.

Excellence ruined by the announced, "If you're done with the quacking duck sex, then Aunt Zahra requests your presence."

Dex was understandably vexed at the interruption, not seeming to appreciate the fact that Deka had been kind enough to let them finish.

Usually, her cousin cock-blocked her every chance she got. Probably because Adi did the same to her. It was kind of a family thing.

"Who the hell is that?" Her poor, modest

man stood in the shower, his hands dropped to cover his junk. A nice gesture, given Adi didn't want to share him with anyone, but she should also add that the man had nothing to be ashamed of.

"This is my cousin, Deka. Who isn't supposed to be here." She added an emphatic glare.

"Auntie sent me. Said, and I quote, 'my foolish youngest child is once again embroiled in something much larger than her instead of preparing to do her familial duty.'"

"I'm not twenty-eight yet. I still have time."

"Time to find the kind of man your mother would approve of? That might be sort of difficult given you're screwing around with *him*." Deka pointed and almost lost her life for daring to stare at Adi's man. Adi's very naked man.

We ssshould take her eyesss. No one should be allowed to stare.

Except Adi kind of liked Deka, a like that would quickly evaporate if her cousin didn't avert her gaze. "Get out. I'll come talk to you in a second," Adi said to Deka.

"You get one minute, but I'd better not hear any more quacking."

"Quacking?" Dex asked when she'd left.

"The sound your dick made slamming into my pussy. You can thank the shower water for that."

She'd never seen a man turn such a lovely shade of red.

"I don't think I will ever be able to have shower sex again."

"Is that a challenge?" Her lips quirked, and his nostrils flared.

"This is not the time. In case you hadn't noticed, we have company and are expecting more."

"Ah, yes, your precious Dr. Kashmir. I guess I should let you get dressed before she arrives."

"And what of your cousin? I don't think she should be here. We don't need any more people embroiled in this."

Yes, the less people who knew what was happening, then the fewer to share with. The hoard came before everyone, even family. "Give me a few minutes with my cousin. I'll get rid of her." And make it clear that, orders or not, no way was she going back to the family home to become a brood mare. The family had enough heirs to carry on the name; they didn't need a baby from Adi, too.

"Why is she here? What was she talking about? What happens when you turn twenty-eight? You're not dying, are you?" He sounded adorably appalled.

Of course he does, because he cares. "I'm not dying."

"Are you engaged to be married or something?"

"There is only one male for me, Dex baby." She winked. "And that's—"

The door slammed open, and Deka stepped in, brandishing a weapon—which she fired!

Pft. The dart hit her lover in the arm, and his eyes opened wide as he slurred, "What the fuuuuu…" He slumped in the tub, and Adi dove forward to catch his still wet and slippery body.

She cast a dark glare over her shoulder at her cousin. "What was that for?"

"You were taking too long, and we have to go."

"Go? Where? And why?"

"Home. Your mother is pulling the plug on this operation."

"But it's not her operation. It's mine." The fact that her mother thought she could meddle just made Adi want to dig in her heels.

"Not anymore. Aunt Waida saw Parker in town yesterday. Mother doesn't want any of us around. She's worried he'll attempt to take you."

"I'd like to see him try," Adi snarled as she heaved Dex out of the shower. She carried him over to a bed, glad he slept, lest he wonder how she was so strong.

I'm really going to have to tell him something at some point. He knew she was different. Problem was, she wasn't sure how he'd handle the truth.

"This isn't a joke, Adi. Your mother is really worried. We all are. Parker isn't abiding by the rules we were taught. Our kind risks being in the spotlight if we're not careful."

"We already were, or did you forget Brand's coming-out party?" Nothing like a dragon ascending for the first time in front of a crowd of reporters. The pictures had gone viral, but society, being suspicious as they were, had no problem believing the many explanations given for the images and videos that seemed to show dragons—actually a dragon and many wyverns—in the sky. The screams of "so fake," and "photoshopped!" meant they kept their secret a while longer, but the time was coming when they would no longer be able to hide.

"That fiasco was contained," Deka agreed. "However, how long before something else happens? It's one thing for the world to suspect dragons exist, another for them to know our family is dragon."

"I'm not ashamed of what we are." If the werewolves could live in the open, why couldn't she?

"None of us are ashamed, but are we ready for the hunting to begin?"

A good point given that the sale of harpoons had skyrocketed after the dragon video incident. "You've been listening to my mother and the aunts. We don't know that the humans will try and exterminate us again."

"We don't, but if they do, they're even better equipped than before."

"It won't come to a war."

"It'd better not because, this time, with science as their ally, we might not have anywhere to hide."

Such serious words from her usually carefree cousin.

"Be that as it may, I'm not going back."

Deka sighed. "I was afraid you'd say that. Which is why…" The hotel door thumped open. "I brought a few reinforcements."

In the end, Adi didn't have a choice but to leave…but Aunt Waida did grant her one favor.

"I'll watch over the male until he wakes." Watch with an appraising eye.

Adi's sudden lunge—hands outstretched to throttle—was probably why her family pumped her full of elephant-strength tranquilizer, sending her into a dreamless sleep.

Chapter Sixteen

Cotton balls filled his head. Filled it to bursting.

Ugh. It took way too much effort to lift his eyelids. Daylight peeked through curtains.

Daylight?

Last time Dex had checked his watch, it wasn't even ten o'clock at night. His fuzzy mind refused to cooperate, so he blinked, trying to make sense of things, as well as lift his face off the pillow soaked in drool.

The sudden appearance of an ugly mug peering at him caused him to utter an unmanly bellow. "What the fuck?"

"Is that any way to greet a friend who wasn't once tempted to dip your pinkie in warm water?" Calvin tsked as he took a seat in the chair by the window.

Calvin? Here? "How did you get here so fast?" He'd called his friend just before his shower, finally ready to call in some muscle. Then he'd hit the shower, only to have Adi tempt him right after and...

Oh. He thanked the gods he laid on his stomach when he recalled what had happened next.

Adi had the most arousing effect on him.

Speaking of whom, he rolled to the other side of the bed and noted the empty spot beside him, a spot that showed the covers tucked. No one had spent the night beside him. "Where's Adi?"

"Who?"

"The woman who was with me. Her cousin came to get her and…" His eyes widened in remembrance. "She shot me with a sleeping dart. That bitch. She drugged me."

At that exclamation, Calvin leaned forward in his seat. "Your situation just became extremely interesting. I think you need to tell me more about your girlfriend and the cousin who goes around with a tranq gun shooting people. How did you find this winning combination? And exactly what was that empty bottle of lube left on the floor used for?"

At the mention, Dex clenched his cheeks for a second, checking for soreness before he realized that Calvin chuckled.

"This isn't funny," he snapped through gritted teeth.

"Says the naked guy I found passed out in bed."

"I was drugged."

"So you keep saying. I miss all the fun."

Calvin would also be missing his teeth if he kept annoying Dex. "When did you get here?" Dex tried to focus on the here and now rather than the fact that Adi had left.

She probably hadn't gone far. Perhaps she was hungry. He could certainly have used a cup of coffee. An IV direct to his arm preferably.

Dex located his clothes and dressed as

Calvin gave him a tally of events.

"So I got your message late last night, but I couldn't get away until this morning. I got into town about an hour ago and would have come straight here, but I noticed that folks seemed agitated. They were hanging in groups and yapping, more than looked normal, so I stopped at the diner to see what was up."

Wearing pants over his junk, Dex felt more at ease. "Between the institute just suddenly shutting down and my landlady's house blowing up, I guess they've got lots to yap about."

"That was part of the news, but what really had them spinning was that local law enforcement found some car outside town abandoned with the engine running, lights on, and the driver's side door torn off its hinges. According to the cop eating breakfast, the body of the vehicle was scratched to hell as if some kind of animal had attacked the car."

An animal, or that demon he'd encountered at the boarding house?

"What happened to the driver?"

"Gone. But no blood at the scene, so they think she's still alive. Just missing."

"She?" Dex wagered he knew who the missing driver was.

Calvin confirmed it. "According to the identification in the purse they found, she was a Doctor Chandra Kashmir. She worked at the institute. She is currently missing, and they suspect foul play."

"I thought you said there wasn't any blood at the scene."

"There wasn't really. Just a small smear on

the car. So they don't believe that whatever attacked killed her, but given the disturbance of the ground and the shoe they found, it would seem she fought her attacker."

Fought and yet still was taken. Fuck. Despite the fact that he knew this was a job, and a dangerous one, Dex couldn't help but feel guilty at what had happened. Guilty because, while he'd been busy seducing Adi and then sleeping off some drugs, the doctor had gotten attacked and abducted.

The fact that it would have happened no matter what didn't make it any easier to bear.

"I should get out there to find her."

"Why?" Calvin asked.

"Because she's the reason I'm here. She's the one who posted the job."

"Exactly. A job that wasn't paying you anything." Because the doctor had suspicions, not funds. "And even if this were a paying gig, the person who hired you isn't in a position to care anymore."

Who would he report his findings to now?

The academy taught to always pay attention to the risk versus profit—and adjust the rate accordingly. But Dex wasn't here for money. "Are you so jaded now that you've forgotten how to do the right thing?"

"Since when do you care?"

Good question. Then again, Dex would like to think he'd not grown as cynical as Calvin. The man didn't see much good in anyone. He'd seen too much evil, done too much evil, to care much about others.

This lack of empathy for the world meant

Calvin sometimes skirted the darker edges of morality. Sometimes embraced death a little too fervently. When that happened, usually someone, like Dex or one of the other boys from the academy, talked him off the edge. He just hoped it never stopped working because if Calvin let the madness win? *Bad things will happen.*

"What do you suggest I do?" Because, right now, he seriously didn't know what his next step should be. Kashmir was missing. His laptop was gone. He might still have the files on his cloud server, or had those been wiped, too? And then there was the fact that Adi still hadn't sauntered through the door.

Did she leave with her cousin?

"You need to call this one quits, brother. Like seriously, pack your shit up before the authorities come looking. And they will. You are associated with the missing doctor."

"I can't leave. I'm not done here."

Calvin leaned back in the chair with a sigh, causing it to creak ominously. "You are such a fucking soft-hearted moron. I swear, if we weren't friends, you'd be dead."

"And that's the truth, brother." Calvin had saved his bacon more than once, and Dex owed him.

"Well, if you insist on staying, then so be it. I'm sure I can manage to wrangle a jailbreak if you're careless enough to get arrested."

"You'd break me out even after what happened in Mexico?" His lips quirked. It hadn't gone over well the last time. The Mexican authorities hadn't been amused in the slightest when the wall of their prison was taken out and spilled almost three hundred convicts back onto the streets.

"Of course I'd break you out; it's the only way I can afford to pay in advance for your future services. You charge a steep price to a brother."

"Just think how much it would be without the academy discount." Dex grinned. Calvin might provide the muscle for operations, but Dex was always the brains.

"More seriously, what are you going to do if you stay? From the sounds of it, everything went to shit. The doctor who hired you is gone. Probably dead. Unless you're related or fucking, then are you really going to put your life on the line to avenge her?"

"This isn't about vengeance. Chandra was on to something. Lytropia is involved in some shady business."

"Was. Lytropia is no more." Calvin exploded his hands. "The building imploded last night, almost as if someone set off some perfectly placed charges. It is now a pile of rubble. Not a single damned thing left."

"And you tell me this now."

"Not my fault you went off on a tangent when you found out about the doctor."

"They're removing all traces. Eradicating something. But what?" What kind of monsters or plan did Lytropia hide? Had they just proven how untrustworthy the shapeshifters of the world could be?

Those...those things are hiding things from us. From humans. Adi hid things, too. Perhaps it was for the best that she'd left. He certainly didn't want or need to be involved with someone like that. So why was he still checking the door, hoping to see her pastel-colored locks and quirky grin?

"If they're wiping their tracks, then you won't find anything here. We both know your forte is with computers, and you don't have shit left to work with. Get your ass back home and do what you do best. You might want to start with finding out who started the rumor that the problems here are the result of anti-shifter extremists." Radicals, who thought they needed to purge the world of shifters and other weird beings.

"Extremists? Really? That's the first I've heard of that problem here."

Calvin shrugged. "Not according to the drama the media is spinning. They're claiming this has been a situation simmering for months, and that LI shut down for its own protection due to threats."

"That's utter bullshit. I never saw anything like that." Oh, how he itched to get his fingers on a decent computer with network access. He wanted to dig. But…if he left, then how would Adi find him?

He compromised by stalling, demanding they have some lunch first because he was starving. He left a note on the bed telling Adi where he'd gone because he still didn't have her damned number. As Adi would say, #hackerfail.

The diner in town buzzed as people rehashed and built on the facts Calvin had already told Dex. Everyone had a theory about the institute, none of them very nice.

Calvin was right. This town—and its people—was a ticking time bomb. Strangers should vacate before fingers began pointing.

Dex returned to the hotel room to see the note still sitting there. Upon seeing it, on hotel stationery, looking so pathetic and needy in the middle of his bed, he made his decision.

He crumpled it and tossed it in the garbage before turning to Calvin. "You're right. There's nothing for me here."

Time he went home—and forget he'd ever met the woman with the green, fire-filled eyes.

Chapter Seventeen

Kidnapped again!

It wasn't the first time Adi had been jumped by her well-meaning family, hogtied, and brought back home—via private jet since regular airlines frowned on kidnapping. Heck, she'd participated in many an abduction when the Sept matriarch demanded it.

This time it was different, though. Adi didn't want to leave small-town hell. As in really, really didn't want to go. Being back home meant leaving Dex behind.

My Dex. The man she'd claimed. A man on his own—at the mercy of the single ladies.

Unacceptable. *He is part of my hoard now.* Never mind her mother had sent a posse to abduct her, supposedly for her own good. Never mind that Adi had some sort of duty to fulfill to her family. *I don't care.* Screw tradition. Adi wanted her human geek back.

Now.

Still waiting.

How she hated being the center of the world and yet impotent instead of omnipotent when it most mattered. *I should be able to have my Dex and eat him, too.* Yes, he'd replaced the cake.

And that's how I know it's love.

Eep. To think she'd mocked her sister. Aimi would never let her live it down when she found out.

Not that Adi would live for long, given she'd defied her mother. First to face the fire-breathing dragon. Not real fire, actually. Her mother breathed what was known as the Dust—a deadly substance that pulverized anything organic that it touched. Mother could take out a good chunk of the enemy with a single breath. Adi on the other hand? She wasn't as full of hot air as others in her family and barely managed to dissolve a limb. But she did have another cool power that no one else in her Sept did. She just didn't brag about it. A secret weapon worked best if kept secret.

Right about now, I'd prefer a secret weapon to use against my family. Her stupid, well-meaning family who'd kidnapped her, meaning she'd woken up alone, in her bed. Home sweet home.

Dammit. Nothing wrong with her other than a bit of a fuzzy head from the drugs. But she was alone, at home, while Dex was somewhere else. Alone.

Hell no. *I need to get back to him.* More than a need, it was a driving imperative, so Adi didn't waste time. Screw walking. She stomped through her childhood home, determined to find her meddling parent.

"Mother!" Adi performed a fabulous bellow that managed to echo as she emerged from the hall housing bedrooms to a several-story entranceway.

A stone balustrade twirled in the space, framing parapets and a grand sweeping staircase.

Gray and white marble streaked with silver. No carpet meant wickedly strange acoustics that somehow held and vibrated in the vaulted cathedral-style ceiling.

"I want to talk to you, Mother," she shouted again. Let her know Adi was coming. It was time Mother understood Adi tired of having to dance to archaic rules.

Silence was her reply. She kept stamping down the steps, heading for the main hall. From behind, she heard some titters as her younger cousins crept out of hiding and peeked through the railings of the massive-sized staircase that swept left and right in the grand hall. It met overhead to form a bridge to the second floor. Such a stupendous space. Adi had spent many hours enjoying, usually at high speeds, the smoothness of the balustrade as she rode it to the bottom.

Hitting the main level, she clomped toward her mother's office. Barefoot. She might have neglected shoes when leaving her room. It took some of the oomph out of her step. Bare feet just didn't scream badass. *Where's a pair of shitkickers when you need them?* Worst part, she knew she had a pair of kick-ass leather boots in her closet.

#epicwardrobefailure.

The door to her mother's office stood ajar, but as she entered, she slammed it with a fist anyway to make it bounce hard off the wall. *Look at me. I'm here!*

As if her mother paid any mind. She didn't seem to care that the center of the universe had deigned to pay her a visit. Mother still persisted in believing it was all about her.

Not anymore. Adi would do what was right for her, not her mother, and she would tell Mother that as soon as she lifted her damned head.

Standing at an impasse, Adi stared at her mother for a moment, noting the strands of silver weaving thickly among her platinum locks. Her mom might be getting older, but she'd certainly not grown weaker. On the contrary, Mother improved her sly games more and more with every passing year.

Thing was, Adi now saw through her mother's act. Like right now, she ignored Adi. On purpose. Her finger tapped at the screen embedded within her desk. A desktop, Adi might add, that was absent of anything but a cup of coffee.

In their house, paper was almost extinct. Paper could be stolen much too easily and copied. The new digital age had replaced it. The fact that electronics could be infiltrated, too, seemed to be a fact her mother preferred to ignore. Her theory was that digital text could be more efficiently wiped if needed. But paper, just look at the examples found throughout history. Paper could live forever. Hard copy also represented a trail. Dragons didn't leave trails. Or bodies, or treasure for that matter, behind. They were efficient that way.

Tapping her foot, Adi could feel her temper rising, a boiling heat as her mother resorted to the same tactics from her youth, relegating her to a certain status, one below her. A subject waiting for judgment.

"Stop ignoring me. I know you know I'm here. You are, after all, the one who had me kidnapped and brought back here. Did it ever occur to you to call and maybe say, 'baby girl, I miss you so much, won't you come home for a visit? We could get like facials and pedicures done while gossiping about the latest trends. Or we could exchange dick stories. I'm good either way.'"

The tapping stopped as her mother's finger still. She raised her head. "Had I contacted you, would you have obeyed? Would you have come and prepared yourself to do your duty to the Sept?"

"No." Adi didn't bother lying. Her mother would see right through it. "Still, though, you didn't have to go all psycho controlling mother on me."

"What else was I to do? Things have become too dangerous for you to remain. Bad enough your aunt disappeared—"

"Wait! Aunt Waida is gone?" Shocking, and yet not as much as you'd think. Aunt Waida was always off doing her own thing. Being married with some boys hadn't slowed her down. When young, Adi didn't understand what her aunt did, only that she disappeared an awful lot. As an adult, Adi totally envied her aunt the exciting job of tracking down potential threats to the Septs and eliminating them.

Sometimes it took Aunt Waida going deep, though, to penetrate a threat. So deep they wondered if she was dead.

"How long has she been gone?" Adi asked.

"She was last seen helping your cousins corral you. We haven't heard from her since, which was over sixteen hours ago." A moue of displeasure creased her mother's fine features. "But then again, she was on a lead, so we've yet to ascertain if she is gone by foul or voluntary means. Knowing her, she's fine. Just being inconsiderate as usual. Always taking chances when she should maybe draw back. Fighting against our rules. In many ways, you're like her."

Me, like my crazy aunt? Just because Adi refused to bow to tradition and liked eclectic wear and out-of-the-box solutions? *Ugh, I am just like her.* "If Auntie went missing, then isn't that all the more reason to send me back? I was on the trail of something. Maybe it's the same thing Aunt Waida was following. I could help find her."

"Find her how? I read the reports, and you haven't been doing much other than fornicating with a human. Really, Adi? And this close to your duty to the family. We're going to have to cleanse your system now, lest you carry a taint."

"You are such a snob."

"Your point?"

"My point is, we both know there's nothing wrong with humans. Or shifters for that matter. They might not be as great as dragons"—nothing was—"but they're not bad people. And they don't deserve to be treated like scum." Especially since she'd found a human who made her feel so good.

"This is worse than I thought. You've been brainwashed." Her mother tsked. "I knew I should have stopped you from going. You're looking for any excuse, even a feeble human one, to avoid your duty. My fault. I thought allowing you to play for a little while longer would help make the transition easier."

"And there's the problem. I shouldn't have to have permission to do what I want. I shouldn't be forced to get pregnant with some kind of sperm milkshake."

"The dragon line must be preserved."

How many times had she heard that line in the last few years? "The Septs have been restored. Look at us. We're all over the world. Hundreds of Silvers alone, thousands when we count the other Septs. How long will we be forced to pop out babies?"

"Until I say so!" Her mother slammed down her hand on her desk. "This is what we do to preserve our race. And don't act like you didn't have a choice. You did. All you had to do was settle down with a proper dragon male, but you didn't."

"Oh, don't you start with that again. Even you have to admit the single guys you tried to throw at me weren't exactly prizes worthy of the hoard." Gross described a few of them. "Did you really want to introduce Cedric's nose to our line?" The man had the beak of an eagle and the laugh of a foghorn.

"Some of the choices might have been less than ideal."

"Less than ideal? For real? They were borderline inbred idiots, and you can't tell me breeding with them would make us stronger."

"Your accusations are groundless. We are very careful with the pairings."

"Careful, and yet I can think of a few guys that are an example of what happens when a mating pool is restricted. What happened to mating for love?"

"What would you have me do? I looked for every single male I could find. They were either engaged, almost engaged, or just not your type. Do you even have a type?"

Yes. He sometimes wore glasses and was fierce in bed. "I would settle for the right guy. Look what happened with Aimi. She didn't settle and found a new dragon."

Aimi found the first living Gold in centuries. Brand wasn't a pure Gold dragon, though. He actually represented a new color with hints of gold. He was the first new family Sept created in eons. He called it Mercer.

Mother still gnashed her teeth when she said it.

"Brand is a special case. I highly doubt there's another like him. And we've yet to ascertain if he is truly a viable mate for your sister. We are waiting to see if Aimi will prove fruitful and, if he does manage to impregnate her, how dragon those children will be."

"What if Brand is able to father dragonlings? What if there are more like him? Locked up in labs somewhere. Dragon mates for the choosing. Maybe another Gold." She slyly inserted her argument for going back. Maybe if her mother thought she'd find a dragon mate, she'd let Adi return to the Lytropia Institute.

"There'd better not be any others. Making dragons shouldn't even be possible," her mother spat, only to sigh a moment after. "And yet, it happened. A conundrum for us all. The Crimson Sept celebrated so hard when they heard a Gold had risen, and are now preaching for a return to the world of man. They are not bothered by the fact that Brand isn't a true-born Gold but one created. Created!" Her mother said in a low pitch, "It's not right."

Because if dragons could be created, and anyone could be a dragon, then did that mean they weren't as special as they believed?

Dragons are awesome. And unique.

Yes, Brand might have been created, but Adi preferred to believe he was the rarity, not the norm. However, with that said, if she could find a few more like him—strong, virile, and male—then maybe the rules for the family Septs could change.

Problem was getting them changed in time before Adi was expected to do her duty. *If I continue to refuse, will they truly force me?*

It had happened before with Aunt Lenora. As a committed virgin, she was fine getting the procedure. It was after that she went a little insane and screamed about the blasphemy of an immaculate conception. Oddly enough, the pregnancy had calmed Aunt Lenora, and she'd popped out seven dragonlings before getting married—to a human of all things—and having a few wyvern progeny, which caused problems within the Sept. Mainly, Adi's mother wouldn't allow the children to visit. A petty win given that Aunt Lenora hosted most of her own family functions attended by all the children and now their families. Rumor had it, Lenora now boasted a bigger dining hall than Mother's. Her human husband had oodles of old money. Aunt Lenora ruled a wealthy hoard.

But back to the possibility of more male dragons in captivity. "The fact that even one was created, never mind the good and bad, needs to be explored. And by explored, I mean we"—also known as I—"should own the secret for the making. Not Parker, not anyone else."

Because secrets were valuable, and that always made the hoarder in her happy.

"You are enjoying countering my arguments," her mother claimed with a sharp look.

"I do my homework. You might think I work half-assed, but I'm rather full-assed." And yes, she slapped hers for emphasis.

It didn't even make her mother twitch. "I still don't see why you should return. There is nothing left there."

"Because they moved. Maybe I'll find a clue to where they went."

"Not in rubble, you won't. The institute is gone. Someone destroyed it like they destroyed the others. Which means we now have to wait for a clue. Your Aunts Varna and Valda are scouring databases and news sources, especially the forums online, for any mention of Parker or his businesses."

"And?"

Her mother shrugged. "So far? They've found nothing. But these things take time."

Time wasn't something Adi had. "Parker is out there somewhere, with more test subjects. And we do have a clue. We now can be pretty sure that Lytropia is a cousin of Bittech. A shell company within another shell. I found them once; I can find the next one, too."

"You found it, and so did your aunts. They've been handling these things for longer than you. I'm sure they can handle it some more while you spend some time at home."

"So that's it? I'm grounded?"

"Until you produce a child."

"And what about once the kid is born? Are you going to give me a loose leash and let me go out and do stuff?" Aunt Xylia rarely left her lab in the basement, but then again, her eccentric aunt, the alchemist, enjoyed playing with her potions. Her children born via insemination? Aunt Xylia loved them, but they took second place to her work.

Will I be like her? Popping out children and letting others raise them? Adi truly had to wonder if she even had a maternal gene because she couldn't muster any enthusiasm for a baby. Then again, there was something coldly impersonal about being implanted with a stranger's seed. Would a child born that way even feel real to her?

My cousins seem real. Deka and Babette had Aunts Xylia and Yolanda as mothers, but no dragon fathers. Not even human dads. Her aunts remained living at home, content in their lifestyles, even if it meant no husbands.

Adi kind of admired that. Or at least she used to. Then she'd met Dex, an adorable geek of a human, with an oddly masculine streak that didn't involve violence, and she had to wonder if perhaps being with someone full-time, waking up to them each morning would be so bad?

"You want to be able to leave? Then tell you what, you give the family a child, and I'll find something for you to do. Something outside this house."

"What if it's a boy? That should earn a bonus. I mean, you want boys, right?"

"Very well. If it's a boy, I'll gift you with—"

"That island you own in the Pacific."

Her mother narrowed her gaze in suspicion. "While a nice piece of land, its value has plummeted since that massive hurricane that left it in a major state of disrepair."

"I know. And I want it."

"Give birth to a boy, and it's yours. But you're paying for the renovations."

"Deal."

Now to get pregnant. With a child. Any child. Because her mother hadn't said the word "dragon" once. Adi replayed the recording on her phone to make sure.

Hope your swimmers are in good shape, Dex baby, because we need to get pregnant ASAP. With a boy. Awesome plan, but in order for it to work, first, she had to find Dex.

#readyornothereIcome.

Chapter Eighteen

Splash. Something hit the water outside in the pool, hard. It took a second more before the alarms started blaring. Dex was already moving, though.

He sat up in his bed, immediately awake and scanning the screen at the foot of his bed. It had dropped from the ceiling and displayed the cameras currently affected by the warning. There were a lot of them, the video feed triggered by motion.

"Rewind, ten seconds," he said aloud. Half the screen changed, showing him what it felt was the best angle on the intruder. Or was it an object? He could see something had dropped into the property from above. Something that performed a sleek dive but wasn't a plane or a bird. Too big for a drone. It glinted silver, flashing brightly for a moment. Bright enough that his eyes blinked.

Splash. When he opened them again, most of the video appeared dark.

Whatever had fallen now took up space in the pool, but he couldn't have said what it was. The lighting didn't allow for a proper view. It seemed something had extinguished a good number of the outdoor lanterns and even short-circuited some of the cameras in the backyard. The black screens, indicative of absent video feeds, taunted him.

What took them out? What was in his damned yard?

Easing out of bed, he debated what to bring with him and settled on the shotgun he kept under his bed. Every boy should have one. Since the shifter outbreak, he'd kept his filled with silver—doused in holy water. It couldn't hurt to cover all the bases.

He tucked the stock under one arm as he strode to the sliding glass door. He was home again, and the basement opened out into the yard by the pool. It also meant easy access if he felt like smoking something herbal. His mother didn't allow it in the house.

Dex stepped outside and immediately noted the moistness of the stone tile. A leftover from the tidal wave generated by the thing that had dove into the pool.

And, yes, he was going with *thing* because he noted movement the moment he entered the crisp evening air. A subtle shifting of shadows that let him know he wasn't alone.

"Who's there?" He didn't really expect an answer; however, he did want to better understand what he dealt with. Was it something alive and sentient having a dip in his pool, or a hunk of junk? Perhaps an oversized drone up to no good.

Water sloshed as the thing in the pool shifted. Warm liquid rolled over his toes.

Live, then. That brought the shotgun out, aimed at the hump.

"What are you?" he asked as he drew even nearer to the edge of the pool. Probably a stupid move on his part, but curiosity made him. Either that, or he harbored a death wish. *What kind of idiot goes to check out giant things falling from the sky in his boxers armed with a shotgun?*

Yet, for all that the situation seemed fraught with danger, and the air heavy with ozone, he wasn't afraid. Tense, yes. His body adrenalized by the situation? Definitely. But not scared. Little scared him since the academy.

A faint whirring sound approached, and beams of light crisscrossed overhead. His defensive drones had arrived, a little too late. It seemed his visitor had timed their arrival for when the patrolling devices would be farthest away. That indicated some measure of intelligence.

"Who are you?" *What are you?* "And why are you here?"

The thing in the pool, yes, thing—its size and the fact that it snorted, a trilling sound that tickled over his skin—heaved itself upward, massive and yet delicate-appearing at the same time.

From the shallow end of his pool rose a fucking dragon, the water sluicing down over its silver scales, the matte finish glinting softly in the beams of light provided by the hovering drones.

"What the fuck?" This couldn't be real, and yet he couldn't deny that he looked at a creature that should not exist.

Then again, didn't I have warning? It wasn't so long ago the Internet had gone nuts with footage of so-called dragons. He'd been so sure the videos that surfaced were a hoax.

Dragons are real? But how? How had they remained hidden so long? And then he saw it. The green fire in the eyes.

They hide among us. And the humans didn't know.

He did. Dex had known there was something different about Adi. Something strange.

The head craned toward him, and for all that he recognized the green in the eyes, the rest proved so different. A giant, sleek muzzle with an uplifted snout, wisps of mist curling from it. Atop her head, multi-colored tufts of hair—or should he call it a mane—flowed in a ridge from the top of her head. The tendrils lifted and waved, floating around her. But freakiest of all, while it had obviously grown in size, he recognized the fucking nose piercing and chain linking out from it that she still wore.

Dragon bling. Fuck me.

There was just no denying the identity of the dragon in front of him. "Adi!" He said her name quite harshly. So very sternly with a strong hint of shock. It was one thing to know there was something different about Adi, something wild and wicked and dangerous. But really...

A fucking dragon?

"I demand an explanation." Instead, she splashed him and trilled a sound that sure sounded like mockery.

"Not funny," he grumbled.

She replied with another noise. He crossed his arms and tried his best to look stern.

The shape before Dex shimmered, almost as if the molecules of her body fuzzed and blurred before drawing tightly together, seeming to shrink down, and down. Then down some more, until the dragon disappeared and a pair of hands gripped the edge of the pool. A moment later, a figure vaulted out of the water, and a familiar pixie-haired girl stood before him. Naked. He stared.

He stared long and hard. He had to. It was the guy thing to do when something incredibly beautiful demanded admiration.

He ogled her nipples so long he kind of expected a good punch to the face.

Adi didn't mind, or so he assumed, given she palmed her breasts as an offering that only served to make his cock harder. She noticed. How could she not given the size of the tent he sported below?

Since she now also stared, he felt no guilt at all continuing his steady gaze of her body. He doubted he'd ever tire of staring. Adi possessed very nice nipples, perched atop a nice handful of boobs. Plenty to cup with each hand. The berry on top proved darker than expected, and it puckered, whether because of the cool night air or his gaze, he didn't know or care.

Those nipples look delicious.

If you forgot they were dragon tits.

A fucking dragon.

"Don't you touch me." He waved his shotgun and had absolutely no effect on the slow sway of her hips as she approached.

"Now, Dex baby, don't be scared. Now you know that I am a majestic beast. The biggest and baddest, as we like to say. Right now, I know you are probably awed by my splendor. Humbled by my power."

"I am impressed most with your sense of modesty."

She blinked at him, looking so guileless he

wanted to kiss her. Because she truly was the most arrogant thing he'd ever seen.

"Modesty is for others. Have you seen me?" She gestured to her body, which meant he turned into a drooling idiot for a moment as blood went rushing south.

She stepped closer. "I am perfect."

"If you're perfect, then what am I?"

What did she see when she looked at him?

"You're the pretty one." She winked.

He took a moment to process it. It made no sense, and without his glasses, he found looking at her made him dizzy. "I am not pretty."

"Yes, you are, and I can't wait to show you off. Put you in some leather pants, maybe just a vest. How do you feel about going commando?"

He waggled the shotgun at her, realized what he did, and set it down. "Not happening."

"What part?"

"All of it. I am not getting involved with you."

"Why not? I thought we were getting along."

"We were. You left." And then she came back a dragon.

Although, in her defense, genetically speaking, she'd always been a dragon. The difference was he knew now and that changed everything.

She's still the same girl.

The inner battle tore at him.

"Don't be mad at me. I wasn't given a choice. My stupid family meddling. I wasn't gone that long when you think of it. Three days."

Three days he'd spent like a loser with his

phone by his side, waiting for it to ring. "I think it was for the best that we split up."

"And now we're back together." Her smile proved deadly, so sweet and happy, he wanted to grab her and kiss those insane lips.

He braced himself against the urge with a simple reminder. "You are a dragon." A flying, massive, who-knew-what-she-breathed dragon.

"You keep repeating yourself. Did you hit your head? My aunt says humans don't handle head blows very well. Perhaps I should get you a helmet to wear."

"I don't need a helmet. And there's nothing wrong with my head. I'm just pointing out the fact that we're different. I mean, you just called me 'human.'"

"Because that's what you are, and I'm a dragon, a silver dragon to be exact. The Silver Sept is considered to be the most powerful of all the colors."

"You mean there's more of you?"

"So many more. But don't worry. If any of the others touch you, I'll pulverize them." She placed her hands on his crossed arms and leaned up on tiptoe. "You're mine."

The words hit him with warmth that squeezed him tight. What he felt for this woman wasn't just something he felt with his dick. She brought out other emotions in him, too. "You're nuts. I'm not anyone's." He most especially wasn't a dragon's boyfriend.

"You'd better not be, or I will have to make them disappear too on account of my jealousy issues." Adi shrugged.

"You can't make people disappear."

"You're right. I can't." She then proceeded to give him an exaggerated wink.

He shook his head. "Why me?"

"Don't worry, Dex baby. I'm sure I'll get a handle on this jealousy thing soon, but until I do, my shrink says you should avoid eye contact with other women. Even the old ones."

He couldn't tell if she was serious or not. She spoke of eliminating people with disturbing casualness. Was that a dragon trait? Then again, Calvin spoke like that, too.

"Why are you here?" he finally asked. "And why did you show me your—your…" *Your true self.* Why couldn't she have kept it hidden a while longer?

"I'm telling you because it's time you know. You asked me what I was. You didn't want to sleep with me until I told you."

His lips quirked. "So much for that promise." He'd lost control and, despite it all, didn't regret it. Worse, he'd lose control again if she didn't put on some clothes.

"It's not your fault you couldn't contain your lust for me. We are meant for each other, Dex baby." She ran a finger down his chest, and he shivered.

"Stop calling me baby."

"I will when we find a better name. But in the meantime… Better get used to it. Because you're going to be seeing a lot of me."

Hadn't he seen enough? The image of her nude body was burned into his retinas. "What do you mean I'm going to be seeing a lot more of you?" he asked.

"We're going to have a child together."

His dick went from excited—yay, a baby—to limp—*Fuck me, she's pregnant!*—to excited again—*Adi's carrying my child. Mine.*

Yes, mine, whispered another voice.

Uh-oh. What did that mean?

First thing, though, how had it happened? "You're pregnant? I thought you said we didn't have to worry about anything."

"We don't, and I don't know if I'm carrying a bun in the oven yet, but I hope that changes soon. I want this kid. Your child, more specifically. It's the only way my mother won't have me artificially inseminated."

Dex knew he shouldn't ask, but he just couldn't help himself—or the hot rage. "Artificially inseminated with whose sperm?"

"They won't tell me. The way I hear it, it's not just one guy's set of swimmers but a couple in the cocktail. The Septs like to stack the odds. It's why twins and more are so common in the family."

"People don't force their kids to get pregnant."

"Dragons do. And I'm almost twenty-eight, which means it's my turn next, unless you plant a seed right in here." She poked her belly. "Of course, our child won't get much help from the family money wise and stuff, given he or she will be a half-breed, and we'll probably be banned from Christmas dinner, but I don't think we'll miss all that much. I took a peek at your assets before flying over, and I have to say, you seem to be doing okay for yourself."

"I do all right." The only reply he could manage given the insanity she spouted.

"You know when you said you lived with your mother and had the basement, I didn't exactly picture this."

This being a ranch-style home built on a slope, the first level belonging to his mother, the lower to Dex. It was over three thousand square feet, per floor, and finished in hand-scraped Acacia for the main living areas, marble and granite for the others. Everything was high-end and expensive. His basement also boasted a wall of windows, making the place spacious and bright in the daytime.

"Are you seriously going to give me shit about downplaying this?" He swept a hand around him. "I think your omission is bigger than mine. Way bigger."

"Don't whine. It's not pretty." She tapped his cheek and wandered past him. He couldn't help but turn and admire her ass. The bare cheeks jiggled just a little as she walked.

She walked right into his place. In his space, where there was a bed.

He hurried after her, stepping into the living room and taking a moment to seal the doors behind him. Then he turned to look. Adi had located his couch and flopped on it, still quite naked, one leg over an armrest, the other on the floor, a splendid tableaux begging for attention.

"What are you doing?" Asked as he tucked his hands behind his back. He wondered if he should have kept the gun. He felt defenseless before her.

She spread her arms wide and presented a

devilish grin. "Getting comfy. This couch is pretty nice. I won't have to change it."

"Why would you change it?"

"Once you knock me up, chances are my mother is going to kick me out of our place, so I'll be moving in with you."

"You are not moving in."

Shouldn't he be adding "I won't be getting you pregnant" also?

She rolled onto her knees and braced her hands on the armrest of the couch. It put her in a leaning position and drew attention to her breasts. "What did I tell you about saying no?"

"No. And no. I am not getting involved with you. A few days ago, you ditched me, without a word, and took off." That still burned.

"I was kidnapped."

"By who?"

"I told you, my family."

He could see the rabbit hole looming, knew he was about to fall down it if he asked, but he couldn't help himself. "Why would your family kidnap you?"

"You ask that as if they would need an excuse. Hello, my family." She rolled her eyes. "Kidnapping, extortion, theft. We're dragons. It comes with the scene."

"A dragon." He snorted. "Of all the fucking things. You're not supposed to exist. I thought we knew about everything after Parker's last confession."

"Yeah. He might have left out a few tiny tidbits. Probably on account of us being the ones best poised to hunt him down and eat him."

"You eat people?" The emasculating note of incredulity was unavoidable.

"Is that an issue?" she asked with utmost sincerity. Then burst out laughing. "Your face. Priceless. Don't worry, Dex baby. I won't start gnawing on limbs in front of you. Unless you piss me off." Her expression darkened. "Then your ass is grass."

"Why me?" he muttered aloud.

"Because you're the peanut butter for my jelly."

"That wasn't sexy."

"It was supposed to show we're meant for each other. Different but complementing."

Shit. He actually grasped her twisted logic for once. He didn't tell, though. "Your obsession with me has to stop."

"No, I'll tell you what has to stop. It's you, pretending you're not totally into me. We both know you're hot for me. I can see it."

His boxer shorts, worn for comfort to bed, displayed to perfection his interest.

"Wanting to fuck you doesn't mean I want to be involved with or impregnate you. You're a dragon, for fuck's sake. That's insane."

"Not really when you think of it. I mean, sure, I'm a lot different from other girls. My awesome factor is off the charts. But I accept all forms of worship. With extra points for the use of your tongue."

"Adi." He said her name on a warning note. "This isn't a joke."

"Want to use your hands, too? Fine. I will also give you credit for dick." Her lips pulled into a saucy smile.

How to resist? She presented herself with impish perfection. She teased him with delight. "Why do I get the impression this is going to end in chaos?"

"Because our passion burns hot," she purred, crooking her finger. He couldn't help but move toward her, drawn by the wiggle of the digit. In that moment, he understood the power of magnetism, as he found himself pulled to the pole of his universe.

Adi is my universe. What a frightening thing to contemplate. But fear didn't stop him.

Their lips met with a soft kiss, and his hands braced on the armrest, on either side of hers.

"If we do this," he muttered between hot breaths, "then we're using a condom." Because while the idea of a child excited, it also terrified. Having a baby with a dragon? He didn't think there was sufficient marijuana in the world to relax him enough for that one.

"If you insist, then you may rubber coat my new best friend. Or we could just indulge in a little oral action." She leaned away from him, pulling her body taut, drawing attention to the indent of her waist, the slight flare of her hips, and the…

"You dyed your pubes to match your hair?"

"I did it during my lockdown at the house. Do you like it?"

How about he showed her how much he liked? He reached for her and snared her slim form, drawing her off the couch. As a dragon, she might tower over him, but as a woman, she fit just right in his arms. He swept her into the air and strode toward his bedroom.

"Where are we going?"

"My bed."

"What's wrong with your couch or the floor?"

"I refuse to get rug or leather burn when I have a perfectly good mattress." A mattress she bounced on when he dropped her.

She squealed, a loud giggle of pleasure that pleased him more than it should have. What was it about her being happy that made him feel so fucking good?

She lay on the bed, arms and legs splayed, not hiding her perfection. She regarded him from under partially shuttered lids.

"Hello there," she said with a husky whisper. "What's a girl have to do to get ravished around here?"

If that girl were Adi? He was already stripping down. The last time they'd had sex, they'd seen all there was of each other. And yet, taking off his boxers, letting his cock emerge, hard and projecting, had a certain erotic appeal. She watched him with such hunger. Such pleasure.

"Mine." When she said it, he got even harder, the tip of him glistening with precum. He grabbed hold of his shaft and could have groaned at the way she eyed him. At the way she licked her lips.

"Lie down," she ordered.

A more determined man might have argued, but he wanted to see where this would go.

It went in a very nice place, considering she knelt between his legs and leaned down, far enough that her hot breath fluttered over the skin of his cock.

A shudder rocked him. A cry escaped him when, without warning, she took his swollen head into her mouth.

"Mmm," she purred. "Salty." A dirty exclamation followed by a hard suck. She let his shaft go with a wet pop.

He might have made an unmanly sound of disappointment.

She heard it and laughed. "Do you want more?"

"Fuck yeah." He wouldn't lie, not with the aching in his cock and the tight pull of his balls.

With a soft chuckle, she dipped back to work, her lips sliding down the length of his shaft, all the way fucking down until they touched the root.

He didn't know how she did it. But he loved it. She pulled back to a halfway spot and then began to suck him, her cheeks hollowing every time she pulled. His hips bucked in time to her sucking.

He felt the pressure building, and then she stopped. With torturous slowness, she slid her mouth back up his cock, swirling her tongue around the fat head. Tasted it. Nibbled it. Made him groan as she toyed with him. He yelled when she suddenly plunged right back down.

She blew him with such fervor and enjoyment he couldn't help but thrash. And then she touched his sac, and he almost came.

"Not yet," she said with a soft kiss to the tip of his dick. "I think I deserve a turn, too."

She flipped around, showing him her

backside before lifting her legs over his until she straddled him. Then she leaned toward his feet, projecting her ass and exposing her sex.

She crawled, backwards, until the core of her, that sweet pussy that he craved, hovered over his face. Sweet temptation. He didn't wait but stuck out his tongue, managing to flick it against her nether lips. Moist nectar flavored his lick, and the decadence had him tasting again, his tongue lapping between her lips. He hummed against her flesh in pleasure, and she shuddered.

She also went back to work on his cock, mouth latching eagerly, her head bobs fast and mind-blowing.

But two could play at this. As she sucked his shaft, he teased the spot between her lips, feeling the quivering heat of her flesh. But it was when he turned his attention to her clit that she moaned around her mouthful of cock.

Having found her pleasure button, he played with it, swirling his tongue around the swollen nub. Since he had the advantage of being on the bottom, he could use his hands, holding her in place for him, but was also able to slide inside her, filling that sweet cunt with his fingers. He fucked her tight channel, felt her clench around him as he rubbed and sucked at her clit.

So mind-blowingly sweet. He couldn't have said what gave him more pleasure, her lips wreaking bliss on his cock, or the feel of her as she came on his tongue, that deep quiver, her guttural moan so exciting he almost spilled his seed.

He rolled them and moved, using her slowness after the minor orgasm to get the upper hand. He grabbed hold of a leg and raised it so that the calf rested on his shoulder; this opened her wide to him.

He thrust into her, feeling the velvet glove of her sex squeezing all around. The aftershocks of her climax tickled his cock as he pumped.

He wanted to come. Come so fucking bad. But he wanted her to come with him. He thumbed her clit, rubbed it and stroked as he thrust and rocked into her, each jab of his cock drawing a ragged breath.

She keened as she bucked under him, her eyes shut, her head thrashing from side to side.

He could feel the pleasure coiling in him again, her body preparing to come.

"Come for me, baby. Come." He pushed the words at her as he pushed himself into her. Her eyes opened, and green fire blazed from them. He was too far gone to care what it meant.

She buried her face against him, her lips latching and sucking on skin. He rode her and felt the pulse of her excitement, gripping him as he thrust.

Her teeth nipped him, and he grunted. She bit him, hard, painfully hard, and yet, it rocketed his pleasure.

He yelled as he thrust deep one last time, so deep, the deepest stroke thus far. Releasing his skin, she screamed and arched. They both came, their bodies joined as one, their climax rolling through them both. His cum spilling inside her.

Spilling.

Fuck.

Chapter Nineteen

Dex wore her mark. It looked good on him. Now if only he would lose the frown—*or I will flip him upside down.*

"I forgot to wear a condom."

"You did." Odd considering he was the one who'd seemed so set on wearing one. She didn't mind them, actually. They just gave a cock a more dildo-like feel. But, so long as it was hard, it worked.

"It won't happen again," he said, sounding determined.

Laughable really. "You're really going to have to get better at lying." She tapped his cheek. "It's okay. I understand. I mean, how can you resist me? I'm awesome."

He growled as he rolled off her. "I'm a grown man. I should have better control."

She rolled onto her stomach and tossed him a teasing smile. "Want me to test it?"

His lips mouthed no, but her mind clearly heard a yes. He stalked away, his ass cheeks flexing. A nice ass, she might add. A moment later, she heard water running, and look who'd left the door open.

Someone wants some company.

Wearing a grin, she bounced out of bed. After sticky, mind-blowing sex, nothing beat a hot shower—where she blew Dex until he gasped her name.

Then she bent over and let him finish them both off. Again, without a rubber.

After he'd banged his head on the wall a few times, she let him escape back to the bedroom.

A while later, she emerged from the shower to find Dex lying in bed feigning sleep. She allowed it. He'd need to gather his strength for their next round of lovemaking. But sleep didn't mean he could escape her. She wrapped herself around him, squeezing him close. He didn't push her away, and so they grabbed a few hours of sleep, long enough for dawn to crest and stab her in the eyes.

"Fix it," she grumbled before shoving him off the bed. Something was muttered when he hit the floor with a thump. A less perceptive person would have heard, "What the fuck?" but she recognized it as, "At once, my princess."

With the shades drawn, she managed to sleep some more, and the next time she woke, close to lunch time by the rumbling in her tummy, she found Dex sitting atop the covers, wearing boxers—as if hiding it would make him less appealing.

I like peeling my treats. With her Twinkie stash, sometimes she liked to go slow, inching the cover off bit by bit. Other times, she was impatient and she tore it off, leaving it entirely naked for eating. She loved saving the creamy filling for last.

Her tempting geek sat there, ignoring her, for the moment. He'd not run, which was good and bad.

The good? He'd not taken off even once he realized they'd had unprotected sex.

Great sex.

So what was the bad?

He'd not run. A shame, because she wouldn't have minded chasing him and catching him. Then ravishing him.

Ravissshing… Her dragon thought she should do that no matter what.

She approached him wearing only a T-shirt she'd found hanging on the back of the bathroom door, one of his. The scent of Dex on it pleased her. He pleased her. It was why she'd looked for and found him. Then masterminded a brilliant escape from Mother's cloying mansion.

The problem with keeping the designer of your defense system prisoner was that the designer, Adi, knew exactly how to escape.

What had proven a lot harder was finding her Dex. Turned out the address on his website was a fake, as was the one for the driver's license she'd found.

However, Adi had sources, which was how she'd found him and, to save time with explanations, made her grand entrance. He initially seemed impressed. Now he ignored her in favor of his laptop.

He totally deserved the hairbrush she threw at his head. It hit him, and she got his attention.

He glared. "What the hell?"

"I expected you to catch it."

"I was busy."

"Always   pay   attention   to   your

surroundings." And most especially, pay attention to her.

"You sound like my academy teacher."

"Oooh, you went to an academy. All boys or mixed? Do you still have the uniform? Will you put it on for me?"

The rapid-fire questions had him blinking. "We are not talking about the academy."

"Why not?"

"Because it's not important right now. What is important is the fact that you're a dragon, but you don't look like any of the pictures on the web—well, except for that recent video footage that was debunked as fake."

"Not fake. That big-ass dragon you saw, that's Brand, Aimi's mate. He's also Parker's nephew."

"Didn't he surface for a party then disappear again?"

"Yup. Once Mother knew we had a Gold, she had him packed off to a secure castle quicker than you can say, ka-ching."

He stared at her, and she could have just pounced him for a squeeze, he looked so adorable in his glasses. He wore a pair perched high on his nose, thick-rimmed and sexy.

"You are going to have to slow down. You are throwing an awful lot of info at me, but I'm not grasping half of it."

"Is this your way of asking for a history lesson?"

"I just want to understand."

"In a nutshell, dragons are old. We've been around since you guys were figuring out that wheels roll better than squares. We kind of ruled over humans actually for quite some time. You worshipped us and took care of us, and we didn't eat you; it was a great deal. Until some brilliant king started thinking it was a good idea to send knights on quests to kill dragons. Back in the day, the royals had lots of freaking daughters. Which meant a shit-ton of quests and lots of dragons died."

"Didn't you fight back?"

"Of course we did, but our numbers back then weren't as great. When you're an apex predator, procreating isn't your prime objective. On the contrary, you don't want to overpopulate. But the problem with that is, when you continue to have infighting that leads to deaths and then a human population determined to exterminate, you end up with a species almost extinct. We went into hiding."

"And managed to stay hiding? How? I mean, I saw you, you're huge."

"Thank you. But my cousin Babette is bigger. She truly knows how to make the most of her size. But her scales aren't as pretty as mine."

"Are you immortal?"

She laughed, a trilling sound that held a bit of her beast. "Not quite, but I am longer-lived than a human. You'll receive some benefit from the bond. It won't make you as long-lived as me, but we've got plenty of years ahead."

"Why are you determined to have me?"

"I told you. You're pretty."

For some reason, that made him blush, and he ducked his head and began tapping on his keyboard again. "Nothing you've told me matches anything I've read online. You look nothing like the pictures. The closest version to what I saw is the Chinese one, but you don't have a chin beard and aren't serpent-shaped."

"We wouldn't be very good at hiding if people could draw pictures of us. But now that digital is taking over, we're getting caught on camera more and more. It's been a real PR problem, especially since some of the older folks in the Septs are old school and think no one should truly know what we look like. They like making witnesses disappear. But then there are others like me who think it's time we cast off the cloak hiding us and shake our titties for the world to see."

"I don't know if that's a good idea."

"Why? Others, like the shapeshifters, have come out, and so far, the world hasn't ended. Which I will admit was kind of disappointing. I mean, we have a bomb shelter stocked with enough for an army to live through any kind of apocalypse."

"If the world knows you're a dragon, then…"

"Then what?" But in a moment of clarity, she understood his struggle, and it made her angry. "You don't want people to know you're sleeping with a dragon. A monster."

He couldn't hide his sheepish expression. "You're not human."

"And you're not a dragon. That hasn't stopped me so far." The idea that she embarrassed him, that he didn't think her good enough, shocked her to the core.

In the silence that followed, they both heard

the woman that sang, "Dex, my darling, I'm going to run errands, did you…"

A woman, older and more rotund than Dex but sharing many facial features, appeared in his bedroom doorway. A woman who could be none other than his mother.

Only one thing to do. Adi sprang to her feet and, in a flash, was hugging the woman, lifting her off the ground. "Mom! So nice to finally meet you."

"Excuse me?"

"I'm Adrienne."

"Who?" The older woman blinked.

"You probably heard Dex talk about me as Adi. His girlfriend. Soon to be fiancée and mother of your first grandchild."

So Adi might have laid it on a tad thick, that wasn't any reason for the woman to faint. Probably faking it, too, given Adi couldn't smell that special scent that normally oozed when prey was vulnerable.

"What did you do to my mom?" Dex sprang from the bed and hurried over. He snatched his mother from Adi and gave her a glare.

And his faking mother couldn't hide a slight smirk.

So the lady wanted to play? She didn't know what she'd just done. Challenge accepted.

"Dex baby, I didn't know you were a mama's boy. That is just so sweet. Too many kids nowadays dump their incontinent parents on institutions, trusting strangers to change their diapers and sponge bathe them. I think it's lovely you've undertaken doing that yourself."

"My mom's not an invalid."

"Not yet. But, at least you live together. It will make it easier when she gets older and requires round-the-clock care. I've heard using enemas can help put them on a schedule."

"Enemas?" The crease of confusion on his brow meant she bit her inner lip lest she smirk.

"Don't worry. They don't struggle much after the first few times. And they soon learn to not take off the diaper."

As Dex tried to grasp his future with his mama—who had her apron tied tightly to her baby boy—his mother feigned regaining consciousness with a fake, "Dex, my darling, is that you? I think I fainted. Something. No, someone"—a heated glared aimed Adi's way—"frightened me."

"Don't worry about Adi."

"His girlfriend," Adi added with a waggle of her fingers over his shoulder.

"Nonsense. Dex isn't dating anyone."

"He'd better not be dating anyone else, or I'll have to give the family lawyer a call to bail me out." She paused for a second and smiled before saying, "Again."

His mother enjoyed a miraculous recovery and got to her feet, hands planted on her hips. Her round, cherubic face—a face meant for wearing flour and sugar dust as she baked for Adi—creased in a scowl.

"You are not fit to date my son."

"Now, Mom—" Dexter, silly boy, he tried to intervene.

Adi stepped in front of him. "No worries, Dex baby. I got this. Listen here, *Mom,* I can call you Mom, right? Or would you prefer Ma? Mine is very traditional and insists on Mother."

"My name is Mrs. Cline, also known as your worst nightmare if you don't get your claws away from my son."

Adi shook her head. "Yeah, that's not going to happen. Let me explain how this is going to work. I'm going to have copious amounts of intercourse with your son. Unprotected. Until I get pregnant, which could have already happened." She cupped her belly and narrowed her gaze. "If it hasn't, then it's only a matter of time before it does because we will be going at it, a lot, while, at the same time, looking for stuff."

"What stuff? Are you talking about drugs? I won't abide drugs in this house," his mother said on a screeching note.

"Agreed. Drugs are bad. Say no to drugs." She whirled to shoot Dex a stare. "And I'm not afraid to make you pee in a jar."

"What is she talking about?" His mother really couldn't seem to keep track of the situation. Probably a sign of her approaching senility.

"I am not senile!"

Oops. Talking aloud again. #needamouthfilter.

"What Adi meant to say is that you don't need to worry about a thing. I've got this handled."

"Do you really? I gotta say, I'm impressed, Dex, taking control, and we're not even married yet. Which reminds me, church or city hall?" Adi tapped her chin. "Or we could always elope and marry on a beach? Then again, I kind of like the idea of living in sin."

"You want to marry my Dex? Please say this

isn't happening." His mother sounded rather faint.

Dex glared at Adi as if it was her fault his mother suffered from a weak constitution. "We are not getting married."

"Yet," Adi added to be helpful.

"Ever!" roared the newest arrival to the party.

Great. Now they had two old women to deal with.

Dex gaped for a moment before recovering and diving for a gun.

While Adi totally wanted to see her matriarch dead, her sisters wouldn't be happy if she allowed it. "Mother, what are you doing here?"

"Mother?" Dex reappeared, holding a gun. Oddly enough, his mom did, too.

That brought a smile to Adi's lips. "And here I thought you were just happy to see me when I hugged you."

"Get out of my house." Dex's mom waggled her weapon.

With hands planted on her hips, Adi repeated the demand. "Yeah, Mother, get out."

"You, too," snapped the woman, who really should be upstairs baking. Adi was getting hungry.

"Me?" It would seem Dex's mom suffered another senile moment, as the gun now pointed at Adi. "I can't leave. Dex is here. Or is this your way of shoving your baby bird out of the nest? Did you want us to move out and find our own place?"

"Dex is staying. You two, on the other hand, are going. Now. And don't come back."

"Are you going to let your mother talk to me like this? I won't have it. It's me or her." The ultimatum seemed pretty simple to her, with a glaringly obvious answer.

Apparently, Dex needed a cheat sheet because he replied wrong. "You and your mother need to leave."

#unwanted.

Followed by a hashtag that said pride. Head held high, Adi turned on her heel. "I'm leaving."

"You are?" He sounded so surprised.

Really? Given all that had happened? She tossed him a look over her shoulder. "Well, duh. Apparently, I have to go find food since the service here sucks. I would have thought a basement dweller was better fed. Since you're not, I'll be back later."

"You're coming back?"

At his dropped jaw, she laughed. "You didn't think I'd scare that easily, did you?" She winked. "This kind of drama is nothing. Wait until you have to deal with my family on a regular basis."

"He will not be dealing with us because you are never to see him again." Adi's mother didn't suffer impatience well. She crossed her arms, the cream linen, stitched in silver-gray thread, pulling tautly, but not as taut as her lips. Disapproval at its finest.

"Never again. I agree." New Mom nodded her head.

"Completely unfit for my daughter."

"Excuse me?" Mom's head swiveled. "Did you just insult my son?"

"How is the truth insulting? I mean, look at him. It couldn't be any more obvious that my daughter deserves better. We are related to royalty, you know."

Good thing New Mom didn't wield a rolling pin; she might have used it. As it was, she didn't look so cuddly anymore.

"It's your daughter who's not good enough for my son. Throwing herself at him like a hussy. Real ladies don't do that."

"She obviously hasn't met the ones who run in my circle," Adi snickered.

Dex shook his head. "This is insane."

"Yes, especially since your mom doesn't stand a chance against mine. She should give in now while the night is young."

"My mom is tough."

Adi looked at Dex's parent, standing on tiptoe, yelling something in Adi's mother's face. "She's got balls. Then again, she doesn't know my mother could eat her."

"Is that likely to happen?" He sounded worried.

"Nah. Mother says old people are too stringy and get stuck in her teeth."

"You're fucking with me."

"If I were, you'd be wearing fewer clothes." She moved toward the sliding door to the yard, and he kept pace.

"Where are you going?"

"I have a date."

"A date?" He stopped walking and repeated it then added more loudly, "With who?"

"With someone who's going to feed me as much beef as I want." She winked at him over her shoulder. "Wanna watch?"

"What are you talking about?"

"Follow me, and you'll see." She skipped out of his house and through his yard, her pace a rapid jog. The fence on the far side proved easy to grab hold of, especially since she ignored Dex's screamed, "Adi, no!"

The metal mesh proved easy to use for handholds. The voltage that usually ran through it? Dead. Lots of the protective measures for his place had been disabled. She'd dropped a little time bomb on his system when she found it. Then added further disarray when she dropped in and zapped it. She might not have much Dust to breathe, but she could give a good zap, enough to short electronics within a certain range.

The smell of barbecue drew her. Dex might own a good-sized property, but the neighbor next door couldn't hide the sweet scent of meat cooking. Someone was having burgers for lunch.

I want some. She just wasn't sure she'd have any time to eat.

Something was coming. She heard it quite clearly when she paused between properties and looked to the sky.

The faint *whup whup whup* of helicopter blades stuttered, the sound of it getting louder. The sun blinded when she tilted to look, but even if she couldn't see, she recognized they were coming in fast overhead. Coming for Adi. *Mother was right; they want me.*

Since she'd stopped running, Dex caught up to her. He grabbed her by the arm and spun her. "Where are you going? You do realize you're only wearing a T-shirt?"

She looked down at the enveloping cloth.

"Yes. Not my sexiest attire. I think I own a bed sheet smaller than this."

"You're not wearing panties," he hissed.

She couldn't help but grin at his affront. "I think you should check to be sure." She tugged his hand, but he didn't play.

A frown creased his brow. "What's that noise?" He peeked to the sky and cursed. "Choppers. We need to get out of sight before we end up on the five o'clock news."

"It's not a media helicopter."

"How do you know…" He trailed off and shook his head. "Of course, you know because this is about you. What do they want? Is it your family again? Come to help your mother drag you home?"

"Not likely. Mother doesn't go for gaudy displays." And Mother wouldn't need help. Adi waved at the approaching vessel.

"Who are you waving to?

"Whoever is spying on us with the onboard camera. Did you know that, contrary to popular belief, dragons aren't cold creatures? Our blood runs hot, so hot," she purred as she dragged a finger down his bare chest. She stopped at his jeans. The prude had stopped to put some on before running out after her. "What a way to ruin a perfectly fine afternoon. I don't suppose I could convince you to take them off?"

"No. And would you stop fucking around. In case you haven't noticed, we have visitors."

"Uninvited visitors. So rude of them to drop in unannounced, but then again"—her expression brightened—"just think, we're about to entertain our very first company as a couple." Because, hello, someone wore her mark. #heismine.

"By 'entertain' I assume you mean kick their asses." He shook his head. "Whatever happened to a quiet night at home playing WoW online?"

"Quiet? Who wants quiet? Pure silence should only occur once you've passed out from having sex too many times. Don't worry." She lowered her voice to a purr. "I'll show you what I mean later. First." She cracked her fingers and rolled her shoulders, limbering her muscles. "We have to say hello."

A ladder dropped from the helicopter, and bodies dressed in black combat gear clambered down. They were of less concern than what flew in broad daylight.

I do believe we just found our demon friend from the other day. The strange and winged imp didn't fly alone. He'd brought friends.

With the odds favoring those with claws, she realized she didn't have a choice.

"How good are your neighbors' cameras?" she asked, stripping off the shirt.

His gaze flicked to her nude body. "I'll erase every single damned tape."

"Awesome. Not that it will matter in the long run. Mother is going to be pissed at what I'm about to do. But, this time, that little bastard and his band of little devils is not getting away."

#dragontime—not to be confused with the hammering kind.

She shimmered, her human body stretching and stretching, the molecules and atoms of her being bending, reforming until she took in a deep breath and felt every piece of her tingle in freedom.

Aahhh. It felt so good to shed that confining shell. All that weight in one teeny, tiny frame. Awfully heavy.

But now she was light. She coiled her legs and leaped, her spring soaring her high into the air, and at the peak, her wings unfurled. Perhaps she imagined it, but she could have sworn she heard a reverent, "Ooooooh."

Adulation—it did a dragon good.

She hovered in the air, feeling the sun glistening off her scales, her splendor out for all to see. But she had no choice; Dex needed her protection. She couldn't do that as a woman. Their greatest chance at survival was getting those attacking to focus their attention on her.

She trilled, a lilting flute of a song, the notes rising into the air and hanging like colored jewels before popping and addling the imps as they flew, the sound waves disrupting the air currents.

The flying demons couldn't see what hit them, but they felt it and faltered, their flight suddenly wobbly. One of them craned its head and hissed, a forked tongue flicking forth.

She warbled right back.

Bring it.

The contingent of imps, seven strong, dove at her, and she dropped, a sudden plummet at the last moment that caused consternation as a pair of demons couldn't halt the momentum and smashed together. With their limbs tangled, they fell and made a wet splatting sound when they hit.

Two down. Five to go.

Wearing a snout didn't mean she couldn't grin. She rolled to her back and did a lazy glide, soaring beneath the imps, who were small enough to move quickly in the air but weren't as fluid as Adi. She moved through the air like water, pulling and swimming through currents, dipping before angling upwards. She dove and weaved through her targets, dragging a sharp nail past. Two more of the demons plummeted, their wings shredded.

She heard an annoyed shriek of, "Leave my baby boy alone," and wasted time looking down to see Dex's mother being carted, arms and legs waving, by Adi's mother. Zahra brought the other woman back into the safety of the house, keeping the human safe. How nice of her mother. What was less nice was knowing there was no way Mother had missed seeing Adi's dragon. #bigtrouble.

Fire burned across her wing, and she flicked her head to see that something dared to slice while she was otherwise occupied.

She didn't have much breath, not like her sister did, but Adi had enough Dust that, when she exhaled, another imp plummeted, on account he had no face.

That left two more imps and some commando types who'd hit the ground and were met by gunfire.

At least Dex had good aim; however, good aim wasn't worth shit against overwhelming numbers. From the road running across the front of the properties, big trucks screeched to a halt, and out poured more men. These men were also armed and began to shoot.

Shoot at her Dex.

She ignored the last two imps as she dove, feeling the air whistle through her crest, her second eyelids shut over her orbs but still letting her see clearly as she plummeted.

She saw too late the guys with the bazooka-type guns on the other side of the neighbor's house. They fired! Fired missiles she couldn't entirely miss. One hit her, nicking her leg. She screamed in annoyance and banked, and a second one got her, the pointed tip digging into the flesh of her shoulder.

Lethargy stole her strength, and she began to wobble then sink.

Dex screamed her name. "Adi! No."

She would have replied, but the earth rose too quickly and...

Chapter Twenty

Dex woke up strapped to a gurney. That was freaky enough. Being naked came a close second—especially since he recalled the academy days when waking up naked after a drinking binge meant dealing with the results caused by a permanent marker and a razor.

He could handle that, though. Hair grew back. Ink eventually faded if soaked long enough in gasoline.

What he found most disturbing of all? The intravenous tube shoved into the flesh of his arm, the fluid being pumped into his system a murky black. Not glowing with superhero neon green or hydrating saline clear.

Black.

Maybe it was just him, but that didn't inspire confidence.

Where the fuck am I?

And who had taken him prisoner? The last thing he recalled, he and Adi had been ambushed. All the security in the world couldn't have halted the miniature army that had converged.

As if that wasn't enough, add in more than a handful of flying demons. Good thing he hadn't run out of the house without his gun.

Adi, on the other hand, didn't need a weapon. She *was* a weapon.

How stupendous Adi looked when she morphed into a dragon—odd how it got easier to say each time. She looked beautifully vicious as her serpentine body flowed and attacked, her movements darting and quick.

She took out one imp. Two. She danced through them as he did his best to incapacitate those coming for him. They'd come dressed for battle, though. Their vests bulletproof, which meant he didn't make a dent.

At the time, things had moved quickly, and he didn't have a chance to truly grasp what happened. He certainly didn't hold back. He might not have emerged as tough as his brothers in the academy, but Dex could hold his own if given a gun.

I took more than few out. However, he hadn't taken out the ones who mattered most, the bastards who'd brought his dragon down. Adi had landed hard, enough to tremble the ground and crush the grass. He began to run at her, panicked as he noted her head wobbling weakly.

Someone darted close to her and jabbed her in the belly.

With a theatrical trill of sound, she slumped to the ground. Immediately, she was swarmed by men with ropes, a harness to kidnap a dragon. They were taking Adi.

The realization saw him sinking to his knees and raising his hands. They shot him full of drugs anyway. Drugs that had now worn off.

"Finally, he awakes." The voice wasn't Adi's.

As a matter of fact, it didn't belong to anyone Dex knew.

He turned his head, craning to peer behind him, and spotted a fellow with silver-streaked gray hair standing in a doorway. News reports with this man's face plastered all over meant Dex recognized him.

"You're Theo Parker. There are a lot of people looking for you." Parker was a wanted man by many people and groups, which meant a shit-ton of rewards. Not all of them wanted him alive. Dexter could retire easily if he killed Parker and gave those buying his death proof.

"Of course, I'm a wanted man. Who doesn't want the man with the balls to do what should have been done decades ago?" Parker didn't sound apologetic for the turmoil he'd caused the world at all. "Who would have thought the cryptos would get so angry when I outed them?"

"Crytpos?" The strange term had a vague familiarity.

"Cryptos, also known as Cryptozoids. The name we use for non-humans. A fancy phrase coined by the snobby scientists to encompass anything and everything they cannot understand. Like werewolves and pixies, and let's not forget your girlfriend, the dragon."

The sly rejoinder caused his blood to run cold. "What have you done with Adi?"

"Nothing yet. The dragon princess sleeps. For now. I'll admit I was stunned by her vehement defense of you. Resorting to her beast side in public... Her mother won't be happy about that. The Septs might have managed to keep hidden after the exposure of that Gold—it was clever to use the truth of his being the result of an experiment to hide the real truth—but the dragons have to know it is only a matter of time before I shove the Septs out into the spotlight with the rest of us."

"Why do that? You're one of them." As soon as he'd said it, a bitter taste filled his mouth. Blame it on the drugs or the realization that, by calling Parker "one of them," he'd relegated Adi to that group, too. But was she really that different from him?

Parker's features twisted. "And there is the reason why I did it. Because I am not a *them*." He practically spit the word. "The cryptids are superior to mankind. We always have been compared to you humans with your frail skin and frailer bodies. So weak you can't handle even the simplest of changes."

For some reason, the direction of the conversation caused Dex to eye the IV. Speaking of changes… "What are you injecting me with?"

"A little bit of this. A little bit of that. None of it entirely human. Most of it toxic usually. The patients who've received it thus far, all the human ones at any rate, died from it. Your body just can't handle the cocktail, but…" Parker leaned forward and grinned, a big, wide, feral smile. "I enjoy trying. You never know when you'll find the right test subject. Just look at my nephew, Brandon. The only one of the test subjects who managed to make it past the deformities and madness to truly become something greater than he was before."

"Somehow, I doubt you'll be getting uncle of the year for experimenting on him."

"Yet he should thank me for raising him out of the filthy bayou he was born in."

The man truly embodied insanity with his indignation at not being thanked for torture. It didn't bode well for Dex. "So this slurry is going to make me great?" Or kill him. He'd survived those kinds of odds before. Hell, his third mission after the academy, his chances of survival had been less than five percent. Luck was up his ass riding him like a cowgirl with a full vat of lube that day.

"Who knows what will happen. The potions never affect anyone the same way. And you are extra special. I've never tried it on a male who's been intimate with a dragon female before. From all signs, she's even mated you."

He wasn't sure what that entirely meant, but given his research—mostly reading summaries of romance novels since no one else really dealt with modern-day dragons—it meant she'd more or less married him.

"You do realize once I get out of these shackles, I am going to kill you."

"You can try, but I doubt you'll live long enough. In a few hours, once we get a few more liters into you, you'll either transform or start bleeding from every pore. It's not pretty or gentle."

"And what about Adi?" Despite the direness of his situation, he couldn't help but ask about her. She was first on his list. A list with three items so far—One: save Adi. Two: kill Parker. And three: find a good detox clinic because he wasn't in the mood to turn into a mystery beast. Although, according to the comic books, the superheroes always got the girl, even the big, hulking, green ones.

"Your girlfriend is the ultimate prize. Not only have I stopped you both from poking your nose into my affairs, I now have in my possession a female dragon. One ripe for mating. If you survive, perhaps you'll be allowed to breed with her. If you don't, then we'll find another stud for the female."

Another stud? Did he mean… Dex began to struggle, his calm suddenly shattered at the threat. "Don't you dare touch her. You'll regret it if you do."

"I regret nothing." Parker laughed, a truly villainous sound. "Now, if you'll excuse me, I have other patients to see, more plans to make."

The door shut with a firm click, and Dex continued to struggle, pulling at his restraints.

Breaking the braided nylon straps by force wouldn't work. He needed to be smart, yet at the same time, he had to work fast. Every second that IV was in his arm was just that much more poison getting into his blood.

He craned to peek at his hand, trying to see if there was a weakness in the strap. Something. Anything.

But he was firmly bound. A concentrated yank on just one, trying to use his body as leverage to pull, didn't loosen it or set him free. It seemed the cocktail didn't impart super strength.

Pity.

Dizziness overcame him, and he shut his eyes, wondering if this was the beginning of the end.

An alarm went off, and a red light began to strobe. Interesting, but not very helpful.

Despite his closed chamber, he heard the muffled *rat-tat-tat* of gunshots and screams. Lots of screams, with some that abruptly cut off.

There came a break in the shooting. He listened, the whoosh of the machines in the room amplifying the silence.

The high-pitched scream started before the gunfire did. Something exploded, causing the entire room, and especially the bed, to tremble.

The shivering of his bed stopped, and yet the shaking in the ceiling continued. The white suspended tiles, high overhead, vibrated, and a bit of dirt sifted down.

It stopped, and yet he continued to stare overhead. He could hear more guns. A full-scale battle appeared to be happening just out of sight.

Once again, the ceiling trembled as if punched and then creaked before falling, metal struts and white panels, along with the crackle of electricity as wires snapped, making him shut his eyes.

"Dex baby! I found you." Strange thing. Dex heard Adi speak. Heard it clear as a bell once the dust cleared. Thing was, when he opened his eyes, he didn't see Adi. Instead, he faced a hulking fucking silver dragon with green eyes.

And then she talked in his head again, and he might have lost his man card forever when he screamed, "What the fuck!"

Chapter Twenty-one

Her mate looked less than impressed with the fact that she'd found a way to speak with him.

Where was the awe that he, a simple human, could understand her?

"Apologize right now," she spoke to him.

"Apologize for having the shit scared out of me? This isn't normal, Adi."

"Normal is overrated."

"Not for me," he growled. "And while we're arguing about it, do you mind yanking that tube out of my arm before it melts my insides into a pink slurry?"

The retort saw her taking note of his situation, and she didn't like it one bit. How dare they try to hurt her mate?

A quick yank on the tube with a claw drew it from his body, and something noxious spilled from the end.

She stuck out her tongue for a taste and immediately spat it back out. *"What is it?"*

"A gift from Theo Parker. Apparently, he wants to see if he can make me into something else."

"But I like you just as you are." Human and all. How fascinating.

"I like you, too; although, I should add, I'm saying this under the influence of some kind of drug." His lips quirked. "But I liked you before that, too."

"Of course, you do. Because I am awesome."

As she used her claw to slice through the restraints, she listened to the distant sound of guns and screaming.

Dex noticed, too. "If you're not the one out there causing trouble, then who is?"

"My family." How did Parker ever think he could take her and not have the Silvergrace Sept and its allies react?

Then again, he might have thought himself safe when he disabled the tracker her mother insisted they all wear.

"So how did they find me?"

Didn't matter. What did matter was getting Dex out of here and to her Aunt Yolanda to see what she could do to reverse the effects of the poison. And it was poison Parker had injected him with. She could feel the dark taint of it through her bond to Dex.

He rolled off the table and stumbled. He also flinched when she steadied him with a talon.

He still wasn't entirely sure of her, but he'd have to trust her. She didn't dare take on her human form now, not when she was so much more powerful in her dragon shape.

Dex wavered only a little as he made his way to a cabinet on the wall. Opening it, he found some folded scrub pants that he put on. It left his chest bare, but it was hard to have lusty thoughts, given he looked a little gray.

"Follow me."

He didn't say a word as she smashed the door to his room open. It wasn't until they hit the hall, with its noisy lights and sirens blaring, that he asked, "How did you escape?"

Not easily. She'd woken, in her human shape, strapped to a table much like his.

In her case, they were taking her vitals, which proved interesting.

They were men, of course, who ogled her body and foolishly believed her submissive demeanor when she woke. They thought her harmless without her dragon.

They'd bound her in silver manacles, locked electronically with thick bolts.

Silver against a silver dragon?

Morons. They'd also injected her with nanobots, or so some doctor had informed her.

"The nanotechnology means we can control your shift. No more dragon for you unless we say so. Better be nice to me."

What a fascinating scientific achievement, with one major flaw. Adi closed her eyes, smiled, and then sent a jolt of electricity through her body. It didn't just kill the nanobots; it shorted out most of the stuff in the room, including the lights.

In the darkness, she'd snapped the silver as if it were nothing. Then she stalked the doctors. The fun part? When she came upon one banging on the door and shouted, "Boo!" He didn't just scream; he peed himself.

Teach him to mess with a dragon.

Once she cleared the room of men playing with things they shouldn't, she went looking for her mate. It wasn't that hard once she closed her mind to all the noise—gunshots and screams and lovely explosions—and followed her bond to him.

"When you say bond," he asked, still following, his shoulder leaning heavily on the wall as he stumbled behind, "do you mean like some kind of ghost leash?"

"In a sense, but it does go two ways. For all that you are tied to me, I am tied to you."

"I never agreed to that."

"I never asked," was her retort. As if she'd ask permission. Dragons took.

A pair of soldiers spilled out of the elevator, but before she could do something about it, something heavy crashed through the ceiling and flattened them.

There went her chance to impress Dex.

Babette shook her head, her silvery mane a wild mess as usual. On her back, a smaller figure straightened and waved—Aunt Waida, alive and well, back to her regular guise of hippie—riding a dragon.

"I see you found the boy. Good girl. Now get him out of here. The charges I've set won't wait for your slow ass." Aunt Waida leaned over and pressed something against the wall and then tapped it. A set of red numerals lit and began to count down.

Adi switched shapes before asking, "Is that a bomb?"

"Yes. One of many."

"You're going to blow the place. But what of the prisoners?" In other words, had her aunt secured any dragons that might be held in the lab?

"The family has freed the ones that were still sane and taken care of the ones that weren't."

"Did you find the golden dragon?" Any dragon for that matter.

Her aunt shook her head. "I thought we might, given the clues I unearthed, but I've been through this place top to bottom. There's nothing here."

"A quick search doesn't mean there's not a clue here that might lead us to the correct location. Why blow this place up? We're in control."

Her aunt shook her head. "These labs and the experiments they're conducting can't be allowed to exist. Their secrets must be erased."

The word "erased," for some reason, struck her. "You're the one who's been blowing the places up."

"I do what must be done for the Septs. And you should, too."

With those words, Waida tapped Babette's neck. Clinging to the mane, Waida crouched down as Adi's cousin leaped back through the hole she'd created, disappearing from sight.

Given the bomb still counted down, it occurred to Adi they'd better follow, except when she turned to look behind her, she noted that Dex was slumped to the floor, his skin an unhealthy shade of gray.

"You were not given permission to die," she snapped, dropping to his side and hitting the floor hard on her knees.

"So sorry to disobey, pixie princess." He slurred the words.

"I knew your nickname for me would be

perfect."

"You're perfect."

"Duh." She tried for a light note, but couldn't help the worry.

He didn't sugarcoat. "I'm dying," he stated. "Run. Save yourself." His breath rattled, and she could feel something tighten in her chest. A feeling she didn't care for at all.

Fear.

Fear wasn't going to win. And neither was defeat. "I'm not leaving you behind." She'd carry his ass out, whether he liked it or not. "The reaper is not getting his claws in you today."

"The reaper exists?"

"Dex baby, you ain't seen nothing yet." But he would because she'd show him. Which meant he had to live, and for that, she needed help, assistance she wouldn't find down here.

Which was why she turned back into a dragon and cradled him carefully in her claws. Crawling through the holes and up the shafts of the installation, ignoring the bodies strewn about. Not letting her curiosity sway her from her path, not with Dex so close to death—and the red numbers counting down.

She left that evil place of secrets, and when she exited a warehouse that seemed so benign on the surface, she faced her family.

A family of dragons. And as dragons they faced her, tall, proud, and silver. Some with hints of color from the mixing of the bloods. Eyes flashing with green fire stared at her, their implacable weight judging her actions.

Risking herself to save a human. Many of

the eyes showed their disdain. But others…others approved, and from them, she took strength.

Cradling his unconscious body, Adi approached the trio in human shape. Her mother, her Aunt Xylia, and Aunt Waida. Yolanda stood sentinel in her dragon, and Adi didn't doubt for a second her aunt would act if threatened.

Carefully, she laid Dex on the ground, the far edge of the parking lot sporting a grassy strip before changing into forest. Bowing her head, she shifted and stood with her hands clasped. The picture of obedience. For now. But the impatience burned in her.

"The human is dying," her mother observed. Except, in this moment, she spoke not as Adi's mother but the matriarch of the Sept, the leader who ensured all followed her rule, even a rebellious daughter.

"He can be saved." He had to be. She couldn't bear it otherwise.

"Perhaps. But why should we? He is not dragon."

No. He wasn't. "He's human. True, but that doesn't make him any less than me. In so many ways he's better than I am. Not that it even matters." She lifted her head and gazed at her mother. "I love him."

"You know the rules. You've broken so many."

The thought that her mother wouldn't help almost made her weep. Then she found her balls and swallowed her pride. She knelt and begged. "Please. Fix him."

"It would be better for the Septs if he died."

Cold, so cold. And her mother wanted an answer.

"I'll do anything you ask, just don't let him die."

Mother then slammed her trap shut. "Will you abandon him and do your duty to the Sept?"

Despite knowing it was coming, she couldn't help but stifle a sob. Leave him?

A glance down at his face showed it looking so pale. Almost lifeless. If she didn't agree to the deal, he'd die.

Either way, I lose him.

Her lips flattened. "I will do my duty."

"Bargain accepted." A deal accentuated by the sudden rumble and tremble as the hidden laboratory was destroyed.

Adi still couldn't believe the dragons were responsible for destroying the other places.

No wonder my mother was so mad when she found out I snuck out to find that last one. Her own mother had almost blown her up.

Why the obsession with such destruction? Adi couldn't help but think it a little extreme given the annihilation took any answers about the missing golden with it.

"You are doing the right thing," her mother said as Aunt Xylia snapped her fingers and moved towards Dex, her steps brisk.

It meant she had little time.

She dropped to her knees and stroked his cheek one last time before they took him away.

His eyes fluttered, and he whispered, "Why did you do that for me?"

"Because I lied before. The world revolves

around you."
#youaremyhoard

Chapter Twenty-two

A ray of sun stabbed him in the face. More like in the eyes, which, even with his lids shut, burned with the radiance.

Dex pried an eye open. *I'm awake,* which in and of itself was surprising. He blinked and took a glance around, noting he wasn't tied, didn't have a nasty IV pouring shit into him, and more surprisingly, he lay in his own bed.

Alone. Yet he distinctly remembered the last thing he'd seen was her…

Telling me I was her world.

He pushed up on his elbows and glanced around. *Where is she?* A part of him knew she wasn't close by. He could feel it like an empty place in his heart.

"Where are you?" he asked, speaking aloud as if it would conjure her.

"I'm right here, baby boy." His mother stepped into the room, bearing a tray.

"Where's Adi?" Perhaps his dread was for nothing. But why did he seem to recall her agreeing to blackmail to save his life?

"That girl is gone. And good riddance. She's got the most obnoxious mother. I, for one, am very glad she chose to leave you alone. She would have been nothing but trouble."

Tons of trouble. And damn it, he wanted it.

Which blew him away. What happened to thinking it couldn't work, that they were too different? Their difference made for a combination that was unique and yet perfect. Adi made him feel things, wild and crazy things. Possessive and protective emotions. Emotions Adi felt, too.

She is right. There is a bond between us. And when he truly looked, reaching for it with his heart, nothing else, he *saw* the tendril leading to her, stretched and faint, but still intact. "She's coming back." For some reason, he couldn't help the certainty.

"No, she's not, because leaving you was part of the deal." His mother looked smug.

Deal? What deal? Perhaps Adi had made a deal, but Dex sure hadn't. *I never agreed to not be with her.* And if there was one thing he was sure of, he wanted to be with Adi.

Did it really matter that she was a dragon?

See, he could even say it now without giggling and looking for a straitjacket.

How dare other people try and decide their fate?

I'm going to get her back. Now he just had to find her.

It didn't take long. Problem was the place he found was loaded with defenses. Fences, sensors, more sensors, a team of drones. Color him fucking impressed. He recognized Adi's hand in the design. A beautifully guarded place. But everything had a flaw.

He found it, and once he did, it didn't take

him long to devise a plan. Calvin helped—after Dex froze all his bank accounts. Funny how that changed a man's tune from, "You'll thank me later," to, "Fine, I'll help you, but sleep with one eye open."

Calvin drove the van they'd hijacked with groceries for the mansion. It ran at night so the family could have fresh everything—especially a ridiculous amount of red meat.

As Calvin, in the guise of the driver, hit the various checkpoints into the property, Dex tossed hacks at the electronics because everything was about having the right hack.

Once they'd cleared the service gate, Dex launched his electronic hacks at the Silvergrace mansion security. He did it so deftly that all the monitoring systems ignored his penetration into the heart of the armed compound. Despite its outward appearance of a house, Adi's home was a very guarded estate—probably because it housed dragons.

When the truck pulled to a stop at the back entrance to the home, Dex dove out of the truck, leaving Calvin as a decoy. His buddy wouldn't stay long. Enough to unload and leave.

Without Dex.

If all went well, he'd have a different route out.

He moved along the house, knowing the cameras were currently looking elsewhere but still wondering if other eyes watched him.

A patio door let him into the house. But then it was anyone's guess where the fuck she was in the place.

After the third hallway of closed doors, he was ready to curse. He'd almost been discovered twice and still hadn't the slightest clue where to find Adi.

"She's on the third floor, west wing. She's got a blue door."

Dex was not too proud to admit he almost pissed himself. Restraining himself from making the sign of the cross at the little girl in a nightgown with silver hair flowing over her shoulders proved harder.

"How do you know who I'm looking for?"

The child—who was surely one head spin away from an exorcism—rolled her eyes. "Oh, please. Everyone is talking about Adi and her human. There're wagers, too."

"Wagers? About what?" And then he got it. She loved him enough to sacrifice it all. Did he?

His expression narrowed on the little girl. "Let me guess, you wagered on me showing up."

"Maybe." The girl batted her lashes with false innocence. "Better go quickly. I hear someone coming."

He didn't need a second warning. He slipped out of the room and located the stairs. At this hour of the night, only faint lights lit the passages. Most of the house slept, and yet, here and there, he could hear activity. He'd better find Adi soon before someone—who hadn't wagered for true love—tried to take him out.

The hall was just as long as the others, with many closed doors, their panels different colors. Only one was blue.

The knob turned easily in his grip, and he

eased in. A gentle glow lit the room, the cause being an aquarium against one wall, the fish in it lighting the space from within.

A massive bed sat in the middle of the room, no headboard or footboard to mark top or bottom. Nestled within the center of a pile of pillows, he found Adi. He couldn't help but stare at her, taking in her perfect features. He'd found her. His dragon princess. According to fairy tales, there was only one way to wake them.

Leaning down, he kissed her.

"Dex." She blew his name softly into his mouth just before her arms squeezed him so tight he wondered about cracked ribs.

"I knew you'd come for me," she exclaimed.

He pulled his head back and asked, "Did you wager I'd come, too?"

"Everything I own, Dex baby."

Because she believed in him. *Us.*

Yes, finding out that the woman he loved wasn't what and who he'd thought she was proved hard. Hard because it made him reevaluate a lot of things, such as what the fuck his problem was.

He loved Adi. Loved. Did it really matter she could turn into a dragon? Did he really care she could kick his ass in a hand-to-claw battle? It shouldn't, because how many of his buddies could hand him his ass, too, with one arm tied behind their backs?

If he could accept that his friends were better and more powerful at some things, then he should be able to do that for her. Besides, there were some things he was better at.

"I'm sorry for being a moron before. I want

to be with you, even if it's fucking nuts. I want to wake up each morning and feel your naked body against mine. I want to take you with me on missions and give you room in my closet."

"And does this offer mean we're staying in the basement? With your mother upstairs?" She arched a brow.

He grinned. "Be with me, pixie princess. Let's piss off both our moms in one fell swoop."

"That has got to be the most romantic thing I've ever heard," she declared, then laughed.

She dragged him down for a kiss, a kiss that he went into willingly. No more fighting this love between them.

This was more than fate. This was right.

Their kiss went on and on, and he thrilled at the way her body undulated for him. Her short nightdress riding up and giving him access to her smooth skin.

It made him ask, "Can I stroke your scales sometime?"

For some reason, this made her groan. "Hell yeah, you can."

Her hands took to aggressively stripping him, but he spared a moment to ask, "Shouldn't we think of leaving?" Before Adi's mother sent in the guard.

She went still under him. "Are you really going to stop this now?" She wiggled her hips, and his cock pulsed in reply.

Fuck it. He'd already defied the odds to this point, might as well enjoy it.

Impatience rode them both hard, whipping them into a frenzy so that, the moment she freed his cock, he was ripping at her panties. She didn't seem to mind. Her legs spread wide, she hissed, "Yesss. Yesss."

When he sank into her, it felt so right. He thrust, feeling her silken channel gripping him, keeping his gaze on her face that he might have the pleasure suffusing it. When she opened her eyes, green fire burned in their depths. Passion. Wildness. So perfect. So decadent. So…

Mine.

Which was why he did that final thing that seemed so crazy. He let himself fall onto her, let his heavy weight settle atop her slighter frame as he kept thrusting his hips, driving his cock deep.

And he bit her. Bit her hard enough to leave a mark, hard enough that her pussy clamped down and almost tore his cock off. But the result?

Ecstasy beyond measure. In that moment of bliss, he flew out of his body, weightless and happy and not alone because he shared that place with Adi.

The most fucked-up and awesome thing he'd ever experienced.

"I love you," he said as they floated back to earth.

"Of course you do," she replied. She snuggled against him, and when she didn't say it back, he tickled her.

"And?"

"And I think you should show me how much you love me again."

So he did. He made love to her again, and again, until she cried his name. Raked his back with her nails, and then finally, spent, on the verge of sleep, she whispered, "I love you, Dex. My mate."

The slam of a door startled them both. Dex could have groaned when he saw Adi's mother glaring down at them. It seemed his parent wasn't the only one with boundary issues.

"What is *he* doing here?" Mrs. Silvergrace demanded with imperiousness even greater than Adi's.

His pixie rolled over and, from under a hank of hair, declared, "He is my mate and, as such, has a right to be here."

"He's human."

"And?"

"He is not a suitable consort for a Silvergrace."

"Not suitable, but still allowed."

Adi's mother planted her hands on her hips. "You can't be with him, not until you've done your duty. You made a vow."

"I did, but so did you. Before that vow, you told me, as soon as I had a kid, I was off the hook."

"Yes, I did say if you had a child you could have some freedom, but I didn't mean like this. Why would you stoop to lowering yourself?" Her mother's moue of disappointment was a mirror of his own mom's—except, in his mother's case, it wasn't the fact that Adi was a dragon that was a problem. His mother didn't want Dex to love any woman more than her.

She'll have to learn to share me.

Adi sat up and crossed her arms over her naked breasts. "You really shouldn't talk about the father of your grandchild like that."

A few people might have blinked as they absorbed those words. Dex sure did.

A certain matron did also. "Excuse me?"

"You should be proud of me, Mother. You told me to get pregnant, and I did."

"Not with a human!"

"You didn't specify, though. And"—Adi narrowed her gaze at her mother—"keep in mind I have recordings of that conversation. Don't make me hire a lawyer."

At that announcement, Dex expected Mrs. Silvergrace to explode.

She did. With laughter. Leaving him more confused than ever.

"You are my daughter. But you do know what this means, don't you?" Even Dex could see the sadness that entered the woman's eyes. "The child won't be a full-blood."

"I know, and I know the family rules."

"What rules?" he asked.

Later, she mouthed at him. To her mother, she said, "Don't worry. I'll be moving in with Dex before the end of the day."

He waited until her mother left before turning to Adi and asking, "What did she mean by that?"

"The Silvergraces don't yet accept half-breed children. But don't worry." Adi tapped his cheek. "She'll change her mind once I tell her I can find the secret for transforming wyverns."

"What? What are you talking about?"

"I'll tell you later. Let me ask you, how do you feel about living on a Caribbean island?"

Pretty damned good if she was there with

him.

Epilogue

Moving out meant jubilation on Adi's part and mournful faces for Deka and Babette. "Now who will help us get in trouble?" her cousins lamented when she returned to do one last trip with her stuff.

"Cause your own trouble. Live your own life. It's time."

Time for them all to stop living for the Sept and choose themselves.

The world was changing, and they needed to change with it.

Perhaps that realization was why her mother had unbent enough to hug Adi and whisper, "Be happy."

"Be happy" didn't mean she didn't cancel Adi's credit card. But Adi fully intended to make her honor the island deal once she saw that the ultrasound showed a boy.

Once the baby is born, we'll start our own family.

A new kind of family with a dragon and a human, loving and living together.

They also started working jobs together because, after all, a couple that hacked together increased their hoard.

Please, you didn't really think they worked

for altruistic reasons, did you?

Explaining her treasure trove to Dex proved interesting, especially the first time they'd gotten a delivery truck filled with cases of Twinkies.

He'd gotten over that real quick the first time she buried him in cakes and filling and then ate him free.

Good times.

Only a few things marred their happiness. One, that bloody slippery bastard Parker had escaped once again. But that was okay. It meant they got to have fun finding him.

Second, dragons were now the item of the day, Adi's appearance over Dex's neighborhood now too much of a coincidence even for the Internet to handle. The media was having tons of fun with it. Her mother? Not so much.

Zahra, as Silver Sept matriarch, was still determined to keep the Silver Sept hidden, but she was losing support, especially since the Reds and Blues came forth and showed themselves to the world—and didn't die. The Greens, Yellows, and others were debating following suit. As if there was anything to really talk about. It was only a matter of time before the world would see dragons flying again.

But would they be safe? It wasn't just the humans dragons had to worry about. Places like Bittech and Lytropia still existed. Experiments still happened. A dragon had been made. Would there be others? And where was the Gold, a certain religious sect wanted to know.

As if that list wasn't long enough, Dex added one more item. "I wonder what happened to Dr.

Kashmir." Officials never did find any trace of her other than the abandoned car and, given the time that had passed, could only assume the worst.

Adi did take offense with Dex when he asked, "Did you eat Dr. Kashmir during a jealous fit?"

As if. "No. There's only one human I like to eat." And Dex was proving tempting, especially once she planted a snack cake on the tip of his dick and proceeded to eat her way to the gooey center.

And as for finding a nickname for him, while she did still resort to "Dex baby" to vex him, it turned out there was one name he didn't mind at all. Mate.

#mine.

*

The sound of gunfire and the last rumble had stopped hours ago, and still, Chandra hesitated to come out of hiding. When the alarms had started, she did the only thing she could think of. She hid.

The metal cabinet proved easy to squeeze into, and she was glad of it because, when the gunfire stopped, something made the whole place rumble. Chunks of debris fell, hitting the floor hard. She cringed as she listened from her spot in the cabinet.

Things snapped and cracked, and she thought, at one point, she smelled smoke.

But in the cabinet there was a measure of safety. A sense of *nothing can get me here.*

Fear kept her hiding as she waited and

waited to see if someone would enter the most secret of the labs.

Eventually, her bladder reminded her she couldn't stay here forever.

What felt like an eternity after the last discernible tremble, she unfolded herself from the cramped space and exited into the lab she'd been given to find it quiet. Too quiet. And she was alone. Then again, she'd been almost entirely alone since her capture a few days ago.

I am not entirely alone. She shouldn't forget who else shared this place.

There was one other prisoner in here with her. How had he fared from the quake?

She walked the hall, noting the heaved floor tile and the dipping ceiling. In some sections, parts of it hung down, and she skirted it, especially the innocuous, dangling wires. If she hurt herself, who knew when anyone would find her? Maybe never.

She'd rarely seen anyone since her arrival. Most of her instructions, and threats, came via hidden speakers.

But she'd heard nothing since the quake.

What did that mean?

Have we been abandoned?

It wouldn't surprise her. That seemed to be standard operation. Abandon ship before discovery. And if they held true to pattern, they'd wipe their traces. Which meant this lab would disappear, along with anything and everyone in it.

I need to find a way out. But before that, she had to do the right thing, even if freeing him would probably result in him eating her in a single gulp.

She'd heard the rumors, read the reports. He

was a killer.

A stone-cold killer of humans.

Yet, it didn't seem fair to let him slowly starve in his prison. Never mind she'd starve with him if no one came to save her or she didn't find a way out.

She really wasn't counting on rescue. Who would come? No one but Parker and a few of the soldiers even knew this lab existed. She could only wonder who'd come to raid the sister location of this place. Obviously, not someone who knew of the treasure hiding not far from it.

Hesitating at every step, Chandra exited the wing holding a few labs and some sleeping quarters. This was where they kept the scientists who got too nosey. At the moment, only Chandra lived here.

At the end of the long hall stood a door leading into the true belly of the hidden facility. She peered around the doorjamb to see another empty hall and more evidence of damage. The only sound was her feet in their thin slippers slapping on the tile floor. A lovely gift from those who'd kidnapped her and brought her to this place.

The gentle hum of the air recirculation system uttered an occasional stutter, a gentle reminder that, once the power was shut off, she'd die from a lack of oxygen. But it would be a gentle way to die. She'd just fall asleep and never wake.

Across the hall was a door that required a swipe of her keycard. It still had power for the moment. But she hesitated before entering.

She'd never gone in there before while he was awake, mostly out of fear. She'd watched the videos. Seen what he could do.

But who could blame him… After what the scientists had done…

Before she could change her mind, Chandra entered the musty space. A cave within a building, within a mountain. A prison for something used to wide-open skies.

A balcony made of riveted metal plates ringed a deep pit, the stone walls of it sheer and glasslike, impossible to climb, not that the man chained at the bottom could move that far. The tethers binding him were short. The drugs they injected him with strong. So very strong. And yet, those drugs would have worn off a few hours ago without someone to administer them.

She peered down into the depths, noting the shadows. She knew from the videos she'd studied just how well he could blend with the darkness. Did he hide now and watch from the shadows?

Would he understand she was here to free him? "I'll get you out of there. Even if it's the last stupid thing I do."

The chamber, usually manned by guards, was empty, but as she entered, the monitors within went blank. Completely dead, along with many of the lights. Systems failed as backup generators died, one by one. Soon, she'd be in the dark and unable to help him or herself.

Back out to the parapet area, she eyed the pit. She saw no way down. No way to help him. She leaned over and peered more intently.

"Where are you?" she muttered.

"Looking for me?" The words were whispered in a rusty voice from behind, enough to startle Chandra into falling forward, into the pit!

The End...but returning in Dragon Unleashed.

More info at: EveLanglais.com

CPSIA information can be obtained
at www.ICGtesting.com
Printed in the USA
LVOW11s0314050417
529651LV00001B/181/P